BOOT CAMP

More books in this series by Eric Walters:

Three on Three
Full Court Press
Hoop Crazy!
Long Shot
Road Trip
Off Season
Underdog
Triple Threat

Visit www.orcabook.com for more information on
these titles. To book a school visit with Eric,
please visit www.ericwalters.net

ORCA
YOUNG
READERS

Book 9

BOOT CAMP

Eric Walters,
Jerome "Junk Yard Dog" Williams
and Johnnie Williams III

ORCA BOOK PUBLISHERS

Library and Archives Canada Cataloguing in Publication

Walters, Eric, 1957-

Boot camp / written by Eric Walters, Jerome Williams and Johnnie Williams III.

(Orca young readers)

ISBN 978-1-55143-695-1

I. Williams, Jerome, 1973- II. Williams, Johnnie, III III. Title. IV. Series.

PS8595.A598B66 2007   jC813'.54   C2006-906670-1

First published in the United States, 2007
Library of Congress Control Number: 2006938765

Summary: Nick and Kia learn that teamwork can be more important than talent.

Orca Book Publishers gratefully acknowledges the support for its publishing programs provided by the following agencies: the Government of Canada through the Book Publishing Industry Development Program and the Canada Council for the Arts, and the Province of British Columbia through the BC Arts Council and the Book Publishing Tax Credit.

Art direction and cover design by Doug McCaffry
Front cover photograph (top) by Barbara Pedrick
Front cover photograph (bottom) by Fotosearch
Backcover photograph by Nick Walters

ORCA BOOK PUBLISHERS
PO Box 5626, STN. B
VICTORIA, BC CANADA
V8R 6S4

ORCA BOOK PUBLISHERS
PO Box 468
CUSTER, WA USA
98240-0468

www.orcabook.com
Printed and bound in Canada.

10 09 08 07 • 4 3 2 1

Chapter One

"Nick, are you planning on spending the entire day playing that video game?" my mother asked.

"Depends," I answered, never taking my eyes off the screen.

"Depends on what?" she asked.

"On whether you'll let me."

"And how likely do you think that is?" she asked.

"Not likely."

"There must be a dozen things you could do," my mother suggested.

"I can think of at least fifteen."

"You can?"

"Sure. That's how many different games I own. I could change to another game if you'd like."

My mother made a little puffing sound. I didn't need to look at her face to know what her expression would be.

"How long before Kia is back from holidays?" she asked.

"Saturday or Sunday at the latest."

"You're allowed to do things without her."

"I know that. It's just that pretty well *everybody* is away on holidays...Jordan, Mark, Tristan... everybody."

"You could do something on your own."

"I *was* doing something on my own until you walked into the room."

She made that sound again.

"I'm just making dinner now," she said, "and after that I'm expecting the game to go off."

"Sure, whatever, no problem." There was no point in arguing.

"After dinner I'm driving you to the community center. I forgot to mention I signed you up for a dance class."

"You did what?" I asked in shock, my head jerking up and away from the game.

"Just kidding," my mother said, and she started laughing.

"You had me worried for a second."

"I wouldn't sign you up for dance lessons."

"That's good to know," I said, putting my attention back on the game. I was doing really well.

"At least I wouldn't sign you up without telling you."

Suddenly I didn't feel so reassured.

"But," she said, "if you don't start doing something on your own, I might find something for you to do, and I don't mean that to sound like a threat."

"Too late for the not sounding like a threat part."

"Just think through what you might want to do. What about going away to a camp?"

"You mean like a canoeing, making crafts sort of camp?" I asked.

"It could be, if you wanted."

"I don't want."

"It could be something else. They have lots of different types of camps. Just think about it."

"Sure, I'll think about it." Thinking about it was a lot different than doing it. Then again, did they have video game camps?

"Just consider possible options and we'll

talk at supper. Speaking of which, I better get back to the kitchen and finish making it since it isn't going to make itself."

"It could."

She gave me a questioning look.

"It could if we phoned for pizza."

My mother didn't answer. She turned and left, leaving me alone in my room with my video game. I focused on the game. I'd only had it a few weeks and it was pretty good...although I had to admit—at least to myself—that I was getting pretty bored with it. Doing something else wouldn't be so bad, as long as that something else didn't involve dancing lessons.

The phone rang.

"Can you get that?" Mom yelled from the kitchen.

"Can't you get it?"

"I'm in the middle of fixing dinner!"

"And I'm in the middle of my game!"

"Your game has a pause button, my stove doesn't, so get it!" she called out.

Why had I ever told her about that pause button? I hit the button, freezing the game in place, and jumped up to get the phone.

It hardly seemed fair for me to have to answer

4

it since there was virtually no chance that it was actually for me—almost everybody I knew was away on holidays.

"Hello!" I said as I picked up the phone.

"Is that you, Nick?"

"Yeah, it's me."

It was an adult—a guy. The voice was familiar, but I couldn't put my finger on whose it was. It had to be a friend of my father or my mother.

"You enjoying your summer?" he asked.

He certainly sounded friendly.

"Pretty much, and you?" I asked, trying to be polite.

"Yeah, it's good to be home with my family and chill during the off-season."

I still couldn't figure out who it was...what did he mean *off-season*?

"My dad isn't here, but you can talk to my mom if you want," I said.

"I'll need to talk to your mother right after, but I need to talk to you first."

"Me?" I was confused. "Sure, I guess you can talk to me."

There was a pause. "You don't know who this is, do you?"

5

"Um…no," I said, feeling embarrassed.

He laughed. It was a friendly laugh and washed away the tension I was feeling. "I'm sorry, Nick, that's my fault. I should have said who was calling. It's me, Jerome."

"Jerome?" I asked. I didn't know anybody named Jerome.

"Sounds like you don't remember me. I didn't think you'd forget me that fast, with us being teammates and all. This is JYD."

My mouth dropped open. "Junk Yard Dog?" I gasped.

"Unless you know another JYD."

"No, of course not. I just didn't recognize your voice and I didn't expect you to call me. It's not everyday an NBA player calls me!"

Jerome played basketball in the NBA, and I'd met him at a promotional event at the mall. He was my favorite player. My best friend, Kia, who was with me that day, had asked him for help in dealing with some bullies who wouldn't let us play on the court at the community center. Unbelievably, he'd come and played on our team and helped us show those bullies up. And, more importantly, he'd shown everybody what being a good sport and a teammate was all about.

6

"Are you keeping up your reading?" he asked.

"Of course," I said. Both my parents and JYD had insisted that it was important for me to read every day even during the summer.

"Cool. And are you playing some ball?"

"Every day, although mainly on the driveway and a little at the community center."

"So how's Kia doing?"

"Good, I guess. She's on holidays right now."

"Holidays? When is she due back?"

"This weekend."

"That's good, because what I wanted to talk to you and her about starts next Tuesday."

"Are you coming to town?" I asked. It would be great if he could play some more ball with us.

"No, I'm not coming there, but I was wondering if you and Kia wanted to come down here...to Washington. I'm running my basketball boot camp next week, down in DC, and I have a couple of spots open. Do you think you might want to attend?"

"What did you say?" I asked in stunned disbelief.

7

"JYD Basketball Boot Camp. It starts on Tuesday and goes to Friday of next week. I'm offering you and Kia an invitation to attend. Do you think you might be interested in coming?"

I was stunned, shocked, amazed and unable to believe my ears all at once. This was incredible, this was just too much to even—

"Nick are you still there?" JYD asked.

"Yeah, I'm here."

"So, do you think you might want to come?"

"Yes, of course I want to come!"

"And Kia?"

"I don't even have to ask," I said. "I know she'd be in."

"I should warn you, though, this isn't your typical sort of basketball camp."

"It isn't?"

"Nope. This is a boot camp. Do you know what that means?"

"Um...we wear boots instead of basketball shoes?" I asked, and Jerome started laughing.

"You'll be wearing gym shoes. Basketball Boot Camp means it's going to be flat-out hard work, hard training, lots of discipline and learning to work in teams."

"Sounds like fun," I said.

"It will be fun...if you don't mind working really hard."

"I never mind hard work," I said, bravely, although I hoped that didn't mean too much running.

"I'm going to be tough."

"Tough is my middle name," I said.

"Great. Why don't you put your mother on the phone, and I'll talk to her about you coming... and Nick..."

"Yeah?"

"Always good to talk to a member of the Dog Pound."

Chapter Two

"I can't believe you're not more excited," I said as I nudged Kia in the side.

"I can't believe you won't let me sleep."

"How can you sleep?"

"Apparently I can't, although I could if you'd let me."

"We're almost there...right, Mom?"

"I think so...not far...at least, I think it isn't much farther."

We'd driven most of the way down to Washington yesterday—Monday—and stayed overnight at a motel. This morning we got up early and were driving the last two hours.

I looked at my watch. It was after eight thirty.

"Camp starts in less than thirty minutes.

Are we going to get there on time?" I asked.

"We're here right now," my mother said.

Mom slowed the car down and we turned off the road and started up a driveway. There was a sign at the side of the drive—The Heights School. The drive curved upward, past lush lawns and shrubs and beautiful flower beds.

"This is a basketball camp?" Kia asked.

"This is where the JYD Basketball Boot Camp is being held. These are the grounds of a private school," my mother answered.

"A pretty rich private school," I added.

We reached the top of the hill, and there were seven or eight buildings spread out. The buildings were as fancy as the grounds.

"I assume we're looking for the gym," my mother said. "The only question is, which building is the gym?"

We slowly circled the grounds. All of us craned our necks, looking for signs or hints as to which building might be the gym. Then we spotted a gardener down on one knee, doing some planting in one of the flower beds. My mother pulled the car up close and rolled down the window.

"Excuse me!" she called out sweetly.

He turned around and got to his feet.

"Could you tell me where the gym is?"

"Gym?" he asked in a heavy accent—it sounded like Spanish.

"Yes, the gymnasium," my mother said.

If he didn't understand gym, I doubted he'd understand gymnasium.

"Basketball," I said as I pulled a ball out of my bag and held it up.

"Yes, yes! *Baloncesto*...basketball."

"Yes, yes, basketball! Where can we go to play basketball?" I asked. "Where is the gym?"

"Ah, ah," he said, shaking his head. "*Gimnasio*... the gymnasium." He pointed up the road. "*Un grande edificio*."

"The big building," my mother said, holding her hands apart.

"*Si, si!*" he said with a big smile. "Big...*grande*... big...*rojo*...red *edificio*."

I could see a big red building at the top of the hill. It looked like it could be a gymnasium.

"*Gracias,*" my mother said.

The man's smile grew large. He said something else in Spanish and my mother slowly, hesitantly, answered back.

He broke into a bigger smile.

"What did you say?" I asked.

"I told him how beautiful his flowers are."

The man reached down and took one of the flowers, breaking it off and offering it to my mother.

"*Muchos gracias*," my mother said.

The man bowed gracefully from the waist.

"*Adios!*" my mother yelled out, and the man waved good-bye.

My mother waved, and we started up the driveway.

"I didn't know you could speak Spanish," Kia said.

"Three years of high school," my mother said. "A second language can only benefit you in life."

"I know some Spanish," I said.

"You do?" both Kia and my mother asked in unison.

"Sure. Taco, tortilla, fajita, enchilada...I know the basic food groups. If I only knew how to ask where the bathroom is I'd be all set."

"*Servicious por favor,* is how you ask for the bathroom," my mother said.

"Great. Now I'm good to go...in more ways than one."

We drove up to the gym—or I guess the back of the gym. It was a big, brick building. It certainly looked large enough to be a gymnasium. The road circled around the side and—

"Look at the crowd!" Kia said.

There, standing in front of two sets of double doors, was a large group of people. There were some adults, but mostly kids, and, judging from the way they were dressed in T-shirts, shorts and basketball shoes, this was the right place.

Mom pulled the car into an open spot in the parking lot. Considering how many people were milling around the door there weren't that many cars in the parking lot—but there was a big yellow school bus parked in the corner.

Now that we'd finally arrived I felt nervous about being here. We were hundreds of miles from home and we didn't know anybody and maybe they were all better players than us and—

"You gonna stay in the car?" Kia asked.

She was standing beside the car with her gym bag slung over her shoulder.

"Of course not." I grabbed my bag and climbed out, slamming the door behind me.

"There's nothing to worry about," Kia said quietly.

"I'm not really that..." I stopped myself before Kia could. She knew me better than I knew myself, so there was no point in denying it.

"She's right," my mother agreed. "You'll be fine."

"It's a gym, some basketballs and a bunch of players. What's to be nervous about?" Kia asked.

I hated when the two of them double-teamed me.

"You're going to have a great time," my mother said.

"I know. I just wish we knew somebody."

"We do," Kia said. "We know Jerome and Johnnie."

I knew she was right. I knew they were both right. I also knew that nothing they had to say would change the sick feeling in the pit of my stomach.

"Look over there," I said, pointing to the far end of the parking lot. Off in the corner sat a large, white truck...the type of vehicle JYD drove.

That was reassuring. "Jerome is already here," I said.

"There're lots of vehicles like that in the world," Kia said, "although not many with fancy rims like that."

Even from this distance we could see the fancy rims. He had special spinners that moved even when the wheels didn't.

"If it is Jerome's vehicle, why would he park it so far away when there are so many open spots that are closer?" Kia asked.

"Maybe he doesn't want anybody to bang it up," I suggested.

"Or maybe it isn't Jerome's."

We stopped at the edge of the crowd. There had to be a hundred kids milling around, talking and joking. The way they were all acting I had the feeling that everybody here knew everybody else—that is, everybody except us.

"Good morning!" a loud voice boomed out, and the whole crowd got quiet.

I looked up, hoping it was Jerome. It wasn't. There was a tall man, an older man, standing there, holding the door to the gym open with one hand.

"Welcome, everybody, to the fifth annual JYD Basketball Boot Camp!" he called out. "My name is Mr. Williams."

Mr. Williams? Did that mean he was related to Jerome?

"I want all participants to go directly into the gym, put your things in the bleachers and assemble against the far wall," he continued. "Parents who haven't registered their children can do that in the front lobby. Let's get down to work!"

He retreated back inside, and the crowd started to filter in through the doors. We were at the very back and were the last three people to enter the building.

"Do you want me to stick around?" my mother asked.

"I think I'd rather you didn't stay," I said.

"Okay. I'll just register you both and then get going."

"Thanks."

Mom reached over to give me a hug, and I side-stepped away. I was too big and too old to be hugged by my mother, especially in front of a bunch of strangers at a basketball camp.

"Are you going to be okay today?" I asked my mother.

"What do you mean?"

"It's just that you don't know anybody here.

Are you going to be able to find something to do?"

She laughed. "This is Washington, DC, one of the greatest cities in the world. I can find dozens and dozens of things to do. There are museums, memorials, the White House...I could be here for a month and not run out of things to see."

"That's good. I wouldn't want you to get bored."

"No danger of that."

"Okay...and thanks...you know, for bringing us down here."

"Yeah, thanks," Kia said.

"Just go and have fun," my mother said.

"We will," I said as we started to walk away.

"See you around three!" I yelled over my shoulder.

By the time we entered the gym most of the kids had already dumped their things in the bleachers and were starting to assemble at the far end against the wall.

"We better hurry," Kia suggested and we picked up the pace.

We dropped our bags and trotted across the gym, passing by some kids who seemed to be more interested in talking and joking around than rushing. We took up a place against the wall, at the far end by one of the corners.

"I wonder where Jerome is?" I asked.

"Don't know. I don't see Johnnie either."

Johnnie was Jerome's big brother—well, his older brother because Jerome was half a head taller.

"I'm sure they'll all be here soon. Jerome did say they were going to be part of the camp too, right?" Kia asked.

"Yeah, he did. It'll be good to see somebody we know."

"We'll soon know lots of people," Kia said.

Kia was good at making small talk and getting to know people. I wasn't so good.

"Have you noticed something else?" I said to Kia quietly.

"What?"

"There's nobody here but boys," I said, saying the last word barely above a whisper.

"There's no need to whisper," Kia whispered back. "They probably already know that they're boys."

"Funny."

"Besides, not everybody is a boy."

I looked around the gym. Everybody that I could see was a boy.

"There's me," she said.

"I meant besides you."

"Yeah...so?"

"So, I just noticed, that's all," I said. It wasn't that it mattered to me who was there as much as I just felt sort of bad for Kia.

"Did *you* notice that we're amongst the shortest people in the gym?" Kia asked.

I looked around. I *hadn't* noticed, but she was right. Almost every kid and every adult in the room was taller than us.

"I just expected JYD to be here," I said to Kia.

"You gotta be kidding," a kid beside me said. He must have overheard our conversation.

"What?" I asked, hearing him, but not really understanding what he meant.

"This is a celebrity basketball camp," he said. "Do you know what that means?"

"Um...that a celebrity is going to teach us about basketball?"

He laughed. "Yeah, right. Do you really think he's gonna be showing up today?"

"Of course, he will. It's his camp," Kia said.

"That doesn't mean he's going to be here today.

Don't you know the way these celebrity camps work?" the kid asked.

"Explain it to us," Kia said.

"Some famous basketball player lends his name to a camp, and then some assistants like these guys...," he said, pointing at Mr. Williams and two other men standing beside him. I'd already noticed one of them. He was popping shots from the three-point line—I hadn't seen him miss one.

"These guys do all the work," he said. "The big-time celebrity basketball player just shows up for an hour or two to have his picture taken with everybody."

"That's not how it's going to be," Kia said.

"Do you see Jerome Williams here right now?" the kid asked.

"No, but—"

"But nothing. You just don't know how these camps run."

"And *you* just don't know Jerome Williams," Kia snapped.

"And you do?" the kid demanded.

"We know—"

"Everybody on the wall right now!" Mr. Williams called out, cutting her off.

A few of the stragglers startled to a trot and a few continued to slowly saunter over.

"Now!" he yelled, and I almost jumped into the air in response.

Most of the remaining kids started running, but two or three continued slowly until they reached the wall. The mouthy kid was right beside me.

"Good afternoon," Mr. Williams said. "I would have said good morning but we wasted part of that by moving so slowly. Before we get started I have a few things to say."

I didn't know who he was, but he certainly seemed to be in charge of things. He was older—even older than my father.

"Let me start by introducing you to our coaches."

So those were the three Coaches? What about Jerome? Was that kid right? Wasn't he going to be here?

"This is Sergeant Kevin."

Sergeant? Did that mean he was in the military?

One of the men—the guy who'd been popping those shots—gave a slight bow. "Sergeant Kevin has been coaching ball longer than any of you have been alive. He'll be leading many of the drills and will instill in you the importance of defensive ball—one of the things that's stood out on any team he has ever coached." He paused. "Anything you'd like to talk to them about right now?"

Sergeant Kevin nodded and stepped forward.

"I've been impressed with what I've seen so far. Unfortunately the impression many of you have left is not a *good* first impression. Many of you looked like you were half asleep as you moseyed across the floor. This is a gymnasium not your bedroom! From now on, you better all remember we don't walk anywhere. We run. Do you understand?"

I shrugged my shoulders and—

"Do you understand?" he bellowed.

"Yes," a few kids replied.

"I can't hear you!" he yelled.

"Yes!" people yelled back.

"Yes, *sir*, should be the answer I expect! Now let's hear it again!"

"Yes, sir!"

"Louder!"

"Yes, sir!" we all screamed.

He nodded his head. "That's better...much better."

"Thank you, Sergeant Kevin," the older coach said. "And now, I'd like you to meet another one of our coaches, Sergeant Josh."

The second man stepped forward. "Good morning, gentlemen...and lady," he said, gesturing to Kia.

Every eye in the place looked down at her—and me standing beside her.

"Many of you know each other. Some of you know nobody. But, as of the moment you walked into this gym, we're all teammates, and as such, you will treat each other with the respect and courtesy that you treat teammates. Am I understood?"

"Yes, sir!" people yelled back.

"I can't hear you!"

"Yes, sir!" everybody, including me, bellowed out.

"When you get rewarded, you will get rewarded as a team, and when you get punished, you will be punished as a team. And that punishment will often involve running and doing push-ups," Sergeant Josh said.

"Everybody, down on your bellies!" Mr. Williams called out.

Slowly, hesitantly, kids did what he ordered.

"I'm now going to show you all how to do a push-up," he said.

"Like we haven't seen a push-up," the guy beside me said under his breath. He seemed to have something to say about everything. I edged slightly away.

The man's back was rigid, his arms straight out; he bent down until his nose touched the ground. Then he pushed himself back to the set position. He did a second push-up, then a third, a fourth and then in the fifth, he pushed off so strongly that he flew up and did a hand clap! He jumped to his feet. He certainly didn't seem that old all of a sudden.

"As you know my name is Mr. Williams," he said. "Although you kids won't be calling me Mr. Williams. You will call me *Sergeant Push-up*."

"What is that supposed to mean?" the kid beside me mumbled.

"Odds are," he continued, "that you are all going to be doing a *whole* lot of push-ups this week. If we catch you walking when you should be running, you'll be doing push-ups."

"If you're not paying attention when we're giving instructions...," Sergeant Kevin said.

"You'll be doing push-ups," Mr. Williams—I mean, Sergeant Push-up—said.

"If you're fighting with or criticizing a teammate...," Sergeant Josh said.

"You'll be doing push-ups," Sergeant Push-up bellowed.

"If you're late...," Sergeant Kevin said.

"You'll be doing push-ups," Sergeant Push-up yelled.

Just then the door at the far end of the gym opened and in walked Jerome, followed by Johnnie. I wanted to rush up and say hello, but of course I didn't. There was a rumble of whispers and pointing as everybody else noticed them too.

Kia leaned across me and looked the kid in the eye.

"Gee, that looks a lot like Jerome Williams, unless I'm wrong," Kia said.

"So what?" said the mouthy kid. "That just means this is the hour he'll be here."

"Eyes on me!" Sergeant Push-up yelled, and

the crowd quieted down. He turned around to watch the two men saunter across the floor. They were smiling and waving.

"You're late!" Sergeant Push-up called out to them.

"Traffic was backed up on the Beltway," Johnnie said.

"Don't care why. You're late, and when anybody is late, we're all late. Everybody assume the position. I need *five* push-ups."

"You want us to do push-ups?" Jerome asked.

He had a surprised look on his face—a really surprised look. Johnnie even looked embarrassed. I didn't think I'd ever seen JYD when he wasn't smiling.

"You're late, you do push-ups. Those are the rules."

This was really uncomfortable. Jerome walked over until he was standing right beside—actually over top of—Sergeant Push-up. The Sergeant stared up at him. His expression looked like he meant business.

"Do you really think we're doing push-ups?" Jerome demanded.

Johnnie and the other coaches had moved in

and now all of them surrounded Sergeant Push-up.

"Rules are rules in this gym, whether you're just *starting* to play basketball or you're a *starter* in the NBA."

Jerome and Johnnie put their things down on the floor. Was this going to become a fight?

Jerome suddenly dropped to the floor, along with Johnnie and the other coaches. They assumed the push-up position.

Chapter Three

"Everybody, assume the position!" Sergeant Push-up yelled.

What did he mean...did he really want us *all* to do push-ups?

"We get rewarded as a team, we get punished as a team. Everybody, assume the push-up position!" Sergeant Push-up bellowed. "Now!" he yelled, and we all dropped down to the floor, including him.

"One!" Sergeant Push-up yelled out, and everybody did a push-up.

"Two!" and we all followed.

"Three!" he bellowed. Doing push-ups didn't seem to take any air from his lungs.

"Four!" I started to feel it in my arms.

"And five! Now everybody on their feet."

As we rose up Jerome and Johnnie grabbed their things and put them down on the bleachers.

"This may be the JYD Basketball Boot Camp," Sergeant Push-up said, "but that doesn't mean that the rules apply any less to you both. The rules are the rules. Am I correct, Jerome?"

"Yes, sir," Jerome said.

"Is that clear, Johnnie?"

"Yes, sir," Johnnie said.

Sergeant Push-up nodded his head. Jerome walked over and gave him a big hug! I think that shocked me more than them having to do the push-ups. Sergeant Push-up didn't seem like the hugging type, but he hugged Jerome back.

"Good morning, everybody," Jerome said. "Thank you all for being here, and please accept our apologies for being late. It won't happen again, you have my *word* on that."

Jerome flashed a big smile that was closer to the expression I was used to seeing on his face.

"We're going to start with some warm-ups," Jerome said. "But here at the JYD basketball camp we do things a little bit differently. Here to warm you up is my really good friend." He turned around. "JY, come on down!" he yelled.

The door at the end of the gym popped open and a big, brown costumed dog appeared. It was JY, Jerome's mascot, a Junk Yard Dog!

"Let's give it up for him!" Johnnie yelled out and people started to cheer.

JY bounced up front, whistle in hand.

"Is this a basketball camp or a kid's birthday party?" the mouthy kid said under his breath.

"You should just be grateful they let cartoon characters in or you couldn't get in yourself," Kia said.

The kid's mouth dropped open, but before he could answer loud music started playing. I looked over to the bleachers. Jerome was sitting there working a soundboard, controlling the music.

"We're going to be having ourselves a little contest...an aerobic dance contest," Johnnie said.

"A what?" I gasped.

"Did he say dance contest?" Kia asked.

"Let's see what sort of moves you all got!" Sergeant Josh called out.

Johnnie was standing right beside JY and he started dancing. Both Sergeant Kevin and Sergeant Josh began to dance as well. The two of them were doing a bit of a bump as they grooved to the music.

"Let's see what everybody's got!" Johnnie yelled.

This was just plain crazy. There was no way anybody was going to—I looked down the line. A whole bunch of kids were moving to the music.

The music suddenly got a whole lot louder. Jerome jumped off the stage and joined JY and the other coaches. The only one who wasn't dancing was Sergeant Push-up—although I could see that he was tapping his foot ever so slightly.

"Best moves get prizes!" JYD yelled out. "Let's see what you got!"

One kid stepped forward. He started to do a really fancy hip-hop sort of step. He was good, really good. A few people clapped and hooted. Jerome stepped over and gave him a big high-five.

Down at the far end of the line another kid jumped forward. He did a moonwalk and then a really cool, running man sort of thing! He was amazing!

"Look at this man dance!" Johnnie yelled, and there was more cheering as the kid continued to make move after move.

Up and down the line people were moving—

some a lot and some just a little. I was prob-ably moving less than anybody else. I couldn't dance.

"Come on, Nick, just shake some body parts," Kia chided me.

I tried to follow the lead of the guy over from Kia. He was moving but not too much. I shook a little and clapped my hands...sort of in time with the music.

The kid beside me started to laugh.

"What's so funny?" I asked.

"Man, I've heard of people busting a move before, but I ain't never seen a busted move!" he said.

Kia broke out laughing.

"I don't know why you're laughing, girl. It ain't like you're doing any better," the kid said.

Suddenly Kia's laugh stuck in her throat. I knew this wasn't going to end there.

"Look who's talking!" Kia said. "You better play ball smoother than you dance or this is going to be one embarrassing week for you."

"I'm gonna school you and everybody else in this whole—"

His words were cut off by a wave of cheering and screaming. Up at the front one of the guys was on the floor, spinning and doing all sorts of break dance moves. People were going crazy cheering him on.

"And we have a winner!" Jerome yelled, and the cheering got even louder.

He reached down, offered his hand to the kid, and as they shook he pulled him to his feet, grabbed him and tossed him into the air, catching him on the way down.

The music got quieter and quieter, and then it stopped completely.

"And can you show the audience what the lucky winner gets?" JYD said, sounding like a game show host.

JY the mascot bounced forward, carrying a duffle bag over his shoulder. He set the bag down and loosened the string that holds it closed. He reached in and pulled out a T-shirt. He held it up. There, in big letters it said "JYD Basketball Boot Camp" with an outline of Jerome, arms raised, forming the letter Y.

The kid pulled off his T-shirt and put the new one on. He raised his hands in the air to imitate the front of the T-shirt.

"Wow, that is so cool," Kia said. "I should have danced better."

"Dancing?" the mouthy kid asked. "Is that what you were doing?"

"Did you think I was talking to you?" Kia asked. "If I wanted your opinion, I'd...I'd...come to think of it, there's no way I would ever want your opinion."

The kid's mouth opened, but he didn't say anything. I think Kia had caught him by surprise. She had a way of doing that.

I looked at the kid. He was around our age but bigger than both of us. He had a short, short brush cut and studs in both ears.

"Hold on!" Johnnie said. "It looks like JY has a few more T-shirts in his bag!" He pulled out a handful of shirts.

"And I found another bag over here!" Sergeant Kevin called out as he dragged another duffle bag—a big duffle bag—across the floor.

"In that case," JYD called out, "I think we have shirts for everybody!"

A big cheer erupted.

JY, along with Johnnie, went down the line handing out T-shirts. Each person stripped out of his shirt and replaced it with the new JYD camp shirt.

"I hope they don't run out," the kid said.

"I think they can count," Kia said. "The number of kids at the camp matches the number of T-shirts required. Not difficult...at least for most of us."

I expected him to react to Kia's comment, but he didn't.

Johnnie and JY continued down the line, handing out shirts.

"Here you go, my man, special order, just for you," Johnnie said to the kid.

He took it from Johnnie, practically ripping it out of his hands.

"Nick and Kia, great to see you two again," Johnnie said. He shook hands with both of us.

JY started jumping all around, being funny, and then he gave both of us a big hug.

I looked past Kia to the kid. He looked surprised, no, shocked, at how they had greeted us. He didn't think we actually knew them.

Johnnie handed us both a T-shirt.

"You can use the change room if you like," Johnnie said to Kia.

"That's okay." She pulled the camp shirt on over top of her other shirt and then, from underneath the shirt there was movement. I knew what she was doing because I'd seen her do it

36

before. Suddenly she pulled her old shirt out of one of the armholes of the camp shirt.

"That's like a magic trick," Sergeant Kevin joked.

"Everybody, put your old shirts and jerseys away!" JYD called out. "And then get back to the line."

"And do that in double time!" Sergeant Push-up yelled.

"Excuse us," I said.

Kia and I hurried off to deposit our old T-shirts in our bags. We were the farthest from the bleachers, and we knew not to walk and not to be last back in line. We sprinted across the floor. I looked back. Our good *friend*, the kid with the smart mouth, was sauntering across the gym.

I stuffed the shirt in my gym bag and we raced back. Despite how fast we moved, there were already a whole lot of kids back on the line. Obviously we weren't the only people who understood how things were going to be done around here.

"Five!" Jerome yelled out.

"Four!" Sergeant Kevin yelled.

They were counting down. A bunch of kids who weren't on the line picked up their pace.

"Three!" Sergeant Josh called out.

I had a pretty good idea what was going to happen if anybody wasn't on the line.

"Come on, hurry up!" Kia screamed.

"Two!" Johnnie called.

"One!" Sergeant Push-up yelled.

"And zero!" JYD said.

There were still five or six kids who weren't in line—including our mouthy *buddy*.

"Everybody, drop to the ground!" Sergeant Push-up bellowed.

I dropped to the ground, along with everybody else in the gym, including the coaches.

The stragglers ran back to the line. The mouthy kid ran right across the whole gym, past all the coaches and took up a spot right beside me. Why hadn't he just gotten into the line at the other side? It wasn't as if he liked us or we liked him.

Sergeant Push-up counted out the push-ups. People groaned and muttered but did what they were told.

I finished quickly. "That wasn't so bad," I said.

"Some people are such suck-ups," the mouthy kid said.

"Who you calling names?" Kia demanded.

"I wasn't talking to you," he said.

"Were you talking to your imaginary friend?" Kia asked. "Cause I figure that's probably the only type of friends you have."

"I got more friends than I can even count!" he snapped.

"Big deal," Kia said. "You probably have to take off your shoes and socks if you have to count past ten!"

A couple of kids heard Kia's comment and started laughing. The kid looked so angry that I thought his face was going to bust open.

"Everybody stop!" It was JYD. "I hear talking at the end of the line," he said, gesturing in our direction but not looking our way. "Everybody down for another five push-ups!"

There was groaning and complaining.

"Make that *ten* push-ups!" Sergeant Push-up called out. "And if there's any more complaining it's going to be *fifteen* more!"

Kia and the kid exchanged dirty looks, both feeling like the other was to blame, but neither said another word. We all dropped to the ground, and the push-ups were counted off.

Sergeant Kevin blew his whistle, and everybody froze in place. We'd been running dribbling drills for the past forty minutes with no stops.

"Let's take five minutes for a water break!"

"Good," I gasped. "I need some water. I think I've lost a couple of bottles worth of sweat."

"Now that sounds attractive," Kia said.

"You're sweating just as much as I am," I said, pointing at her sweat-soaked T-shirt.

"That's where you're wrong. I don't sweat, I *glow*."

"In that case you're glowing so bright we could turn off the overhead lights."

We joined in a lineup to get bottles of water. We shuffled forward. JY and Johnnie were passing them out.

"Working hard?" Johnnie asked Kia.

"Hard enough to work up a good sweat," I said, "or a good glow."

"Kia, Nick, come on over here!" JYD called. He was standing beside the Sergeant. We trotted over, water bottles in hand.

"I want you to meet somebody," JYD said, gesturing to Sergeant Push-up.

"We sort of already know who he is," Kia said.

"But do you two know *who* this gentleman is?" Jerome asked.

"Sergeant Push-up," Kia said.

JYD chuckled. "That's one of his names. This is the man that taught me everything I know about basketball."

"But I thought your father taught you everything..." Now it all made sense.

"This *is* my father...Mr. Johnnie Williams Junior."

He shook both our hands. "Jerome told me all about you two," Mr. Williams said.

"He has?" I asked.

"Sure, I always tell my father about my Dog Pound members," JYD said.

"And we know a lot about you too," Kia said.

"How's that?" Mr. Williams asked.

"Jerome and Johnnie talk about you...and how you taught them basketball."

"And about life," I added.

Mr. Williams smiled. "The life part is what makes me the happiest. I'm proud of what my boys have done on the court, but a lot more proud of what they do off the court."

"Can I ask a question?" Kia asked.

"Sure," he said.

41

"We're always willing to answer questions," JYD said.

"I was just wondering...please don't take offence or anything," she said.

"Now you got me interested. What are you going to ask that could get me offended?" JYD asked.

"Well...I was just wondering...are you going to be here much this week?"

"Of course, I am," he said. "It's my camp."

"Yeah, I know, but we heard that some celebrities only show up for a few hours," Kia explained.

"That's not the way we run things around here," Jerome said. "I'll be here all day, every day, from the start to the finish."

"Could I ask a question too?" I asked.

"Of course," JYD said.

"Since you're going to be here every day, from the start to the finish...I was just wondering, this morning, were you and Johnnie really late?"

"You saw us come into the gym," JYD said.

"I saw you come in, but were you really late?" I asked.

"Why would you think differently?" Sergeant—Mr. Williams—said.

"It's just that we saw an Escalade in the parking lot that looked like yours," I said.

"There are lots of Escalades in the world," JYD replied.

"I said that," Kia agreed.

"Anyway, why would you think that they'd come in late if they were already here?" Mr. Williams asked.

"To set an example," I said. "You wanted everybody to see that the rules are the rules," I answered. "For everybody."

"Exactly! That makes perfect sense!" Kia said as she suddenly realized what I was saying. "Every kid here got to witness, with their own eyes, the fact that nobody is going to get away with breaking the rules...even Jerome Junk Yard Dog Williams has to answer if he does wrong."

Neither of the Williams answered right away. Were they angry or upset about what we'd suggested?

Mr. Williams turned to his son. "You weren't telling lies. These two *are* sharp."

"Then we're right?" Kia asked.

"Ssshhhhhh!" JYD said. "Keep your voice down."

"We were right?" Kia whispered.

43

"You were right, but you can't tell anybody," Mr. Williams said.

"We won't tell anybody," I assured him.

"You can trust us to keep it a secret," Kia said.

"Jerome?" Mr. Williams asked. "What do you think, can they keep a secret?"

"If they give their word then you can bet your life on it."

"All I need to know. Now, enough talking. It's time to play some ball."

Mr. Williams's expression suddenly got tough looking. I knew what was happening—Mr. Williams was becoming Sergeant Push-up again. He blew his whistle.

"Everybody down to the end line!" he called out, and everybody started into motion. "And let's have no walking!"

Chapter Four

I'd been watching the clock pretty closely for the last thirty minutes. It was almost three o'clock, almost time for the first day to end. It had been fun, and I'd learned a whole lot, but I didn't know how much more I had in the tank. When we weren't doing drills, we were running, and when we weren't running, we were down on the ground doing push-ups—or sit-ups. I'd never been worked this hard in my whole life.

Parents—including my mother who had arrived ten minutes earlier—were filtering into the gym and taking spots in the bleachers, waiting and watching the last few minutes of the day.

"Bring it in!" Sergeant Kevin yelled. "Everybody into the center of the gym!"

"And no dawdling!" JYD added, causing people to rush into the middle.

"Take a seat."

We all sat on the floor with JYD standing in the middle. It felt good to be sitting. Lying down would have been even better. I figured that the second my head hit the pillow in the motel tonight I'd be sound asleep.

"I want everybody to turn slightly to their right and give a pat on the back to the person sitting beside you," JYD said.

I gave a tentative pat on the back to the guy beside me while another guy pounded me on the back.

"You have all survived day one of basketball boot camp," JYD said. "I'd like to tell you that it only gets easier from here but it doesn't."

"That's the truth," Johnnie said, agreeing with his brother.

"Does anybody know how many push-ups we did today?" Sergeant Josh asked.

"About a million," one kid volunteered.

"Close. One hundred and eighty-seven," Sergeant Push-up said.

I didn't know if that was right, but if anybody knew, it had to be him.

"That's one hundred and eighty-seven push-ups that were done because one of you didn't arrive on time, took too long getting a drink, didn't listen to instructions, or were talking when you should have been listening. Remember, God gave you two ears and one mouth because you're supposed to be listening twice as much as you talk."

"I want you all to go home, get some food into you, get a good night's sleep and come on back here, bright and early tomorrow morning," JYD said. "Now, everybody stand up, put a hand into the middle."

Everybody jumped to their feet and pushed in, trying to make a pile of hands in the middle on top of Jerome's big mitt. There was a mass of bodies—the sweaty bodies of a whole bunch of strangers—all crushed in together.

"Okay, everybody, on three yell, 'Hard work,'" JYD said. "One, two, three—"

"Hard work!" we all screamed and threw our hands into the air.

There was a burst of conversations and laughter as everybody started toward the bleachers. It was like all the words that hadn't been used throughout the day rushed out.

Interestingly that was the only rush. Nobody was moving very fast. Maybe it was because we were too tired or just reacting to the fact that we couldn't take our time during the day—at least not without paying for it in push-ups.

"So did you have a good time?" my mother asked as we reached the bleachers.

"Good, but tiring," I said.

"Tiring doesn't start to describe it. I'm bagged," Kia said.

"Too bagged for a little sightseeing?" my mother asked.

"The only sight I want to see is a hotel room," Kia said.

"No, first dinner, and then the hotel room," I added. "Although, maybe we could take a nap before dinner."

"Sounds like they really worked you today," she said.

"I'm exhausted," I said.

"That's good to hear," came a voice from behind me. It was Jerome.

"We're not complaining!" I protested.

"Didn't think you were," JYD said. He and my mother shook hands and exchanged greetings.

"We like to think that we work the kids pretty hard," JYD said.

"No pain, no gain, right?" I said.

"That's what I hear, although it's pretty hard to believe that when you're going through the pain," JYD said.

"We can handle it," Kia said.

JYD smiled. "Never had any doubts about that. Are you having fun?"

"Actually, a lot of fun," I said.

"Despite how tough it is?" he asked.

"Maybe *because* of how tough it is," I said.

He gave me a questioning look.

"It's not just a camp on learning about basketball," I said.

"And we are learning," Kia added.

"But we're being pushed to try harder, to be more than we were when we walked in the door," I said.

JYD put a hand on my shoulder. "That's good to hear. We like to think that this camp is about more than just learning about basketball."

"I was wondering," my mother said, "if you can tell us where we could find a good hotel close to here."

"I could, but I won't be doing that," he said.

What did he mean?

"You three are going to be my guests. You'll be staying at my home with my wife and me."

"Your house?" I gasped.

"It would be rude of me to invite you all the way down here to my boot camp and have you stay in some hotel."

"That's a kind offer, but we can stay at a hotel. We don't want to put you out," my mother said.

"That won't be a problem at all. Johnnie and Sergeant—well, my younger brother Joshua—are staying with us as well."

"Do you still have space for us too?" my mother asked.

"There's room for everybody," JYD said.

I was thinking that he probably did have a pretty big house—he was in the NBA.

"I don't know...we really don't want to impose," said my mother.

"You won't be imposing."

"Well..."

"Please, Mom," I pleaded. How cool would it be to stay at Jerome's house.

"Yeah, please," Kia added.

She looked at both of us and then up at JYD. "Thank you for your very kind offer. We'd be happy to stay with you and your family."

Chapter Five

"And turn left here," I said as I read out the directions to my mother. "This is the street."

She slowed the car down and turned.

"This is quite the neighborhood," Kia said.

"The houses look really huge...at least what I can see of most of them," I said.

The properties were so large and there were so many big trees that most of the houses were hidden from the road.

"I've been following the numbers. It isn't too much farther. You should slow down. It might even be the next house," Kia said.

My mother slowed down. On the left we were passing a long stone wall. I knew there was a house up there somewhere but it was out of sight. Up ahead there was a driveway.

"Can you see the address?" I asked.

Kia leaned forward and looked through the windshield. "Four...seven...six...that's it!"

Mom pulled the car into the driveway, stopping in front of a gigantic metal gate. She rolled down her window and pushed a little button— a sort of doorbell. There was a buzzing sound.

"Hello," called out a female voice over an intercom.

"Hi, we're here at the invitation of Jerome. My name is—"

"You're Kia and Nick and his mother. I can *see* who you are," the voice responded. "Look at the camera and wave!"

I looked up. A few feet above the buzzer was a camera, pointed right at us. I gave a weak little wave.

"Come on in," the voice said. Whoever it was, she sounded friendly.

Slowly the big metal gate opened, and we drove through. The driveway was long and wound its way across a beautiful lawn. The house—the big house—was up at the top behind a grove of trees.

"Wow, quite the place," Kia said.

"I don't think he's going to make us sleep

53

on the couch," I said. "I figure he's got lots of room."

We came to a stop at the big, double front doors of the house. As we climbed out of the car the front doors opened. Out came a woman, holding a little toddler, and a teenage girl, holding the hand of another little girl.

"Hello," the woman said. Her voice was soft and she was smiling. "I'm Nikkollette, Jerome's wife."

"Pleased to meet you," my mother said, and they did a sort of ladylike handshake thing.

Nikkollette then shook hands with both Kia and me.

"I feel a little uncomfortable just dropping in on you like this," my mother said.

"You shouldn't. Jerome is always inviting people to stay with us. We love the company! Now let me introduce you to our girls."

"Hi, I'm Sherea," the teenager said. "And these two little angels are my sisters. The baby is Giselle, she's three."

Giselle turned away and sort of snuggled her face into her mother to hide.

"She's a bit shy," Sherea said. "And this is Gabby."

"Gabrielle," the little girl said defiantly. She shook her hand loose from her sister and glared up at her.

Sherea laughed. "Yes, *Gabrielle*, and you can see that she has *no* problem expressing herself. She's not shy."

"I'm not shy...I'm Gabrielle."

"Pleased to meet you, Gabrielle," Kia said as she bent to the girl's eye level.

"Pleased to meet you too," she replied. She was one confident little kid.

"Sherea," Nikkollette said, "how about if you give everybody a tour while I finish making dinner."

"Sure."

"How about if I help you finish making dinner," my mother suggested.

"That's a lovely offer, but you're our guest, and I just want you to make yourself comfortable."

"Helping you make supper would make me feel comfortable...and at home."

"In that case," Nikkollette said, "I'd appreciate your help and your company. We'll get everything ready and then wait for Jerome to arrive."

"He's not here yet?" I asked.

"He and Johnnie, their father, and of course, Joshua, are driving kids home from the camp. It could be a while. Once Jerome starts talking, or worse, signing autographs, there's no telling how long he'll be," she said.

"Even when he should be hurrying," Sherea said. "We're always late whenever we're going almost anywhere."

"Jerome just has trouble saying no to people," Nikkollette said.

"You can say that again," Sherea said.

"And his girls should be grateful for that," Nikkollette said.

Sherea gave a coy smile.

"All the girls have to do is smile and say 'Please Daddy,' and he just melts. The man is the biggest softy in the world. He gets that from his father," Nikkollette said.

"From Sergeant Push-up?" I asked in shock.

"Don't let his act at the camp fool you. He's a strong man; he believes in discipline and working hard, but he's just as soft, just as big a kid as his own kids." She paused. "You'll see more of that side tonight."

"Tonight?" Kia asked.

"He's joining us for dinner."

"Dinner...we're not going to have to do push-ups if we have bad table manners, are we?" I asked.

Everybody laughed. Actually I hadn't meant that as a joke.

"No push-ups, but you probably will have to play Scrabble with him or drive the go-carts," Sherea said.

"I love go-carts!" I said.

"So does Jerome. He owns five of them."

"That's incredible," Kia said.

"Do you have a track near here?" I asked.

"Not *near* here. Here," Sherea said, pointing to the grounds.

What was she talking about? They couldn't possibly have a go-cart track right on the property...could they?

"You have a track, right here?" I asked in astonishment.

"It's quite a nice track. With all the curves it's about a half a mile long."

I shook my head in disbelief.

"I couldn't imagine there would be many homes that feature their own go-cart track," Nikkollette said.

"Or an official NBA-sized basketball court," Sherea added.

"You're joking, right?" I asked.

"No joke. I'll show you both on the tour."

"How about if you start with the go-carts and track, and then you finish up in the house with the arcade?" Nikkollette suggested.

"Arcade?" Kia asked.

"I told you. Jerome's just a big kid and big kids need lots of toys."

"Come on," Sherea said.

Kia and I trailed after her. Gabby—Gabrielle—was still holding onto her sister's hand.

The meal was almost finished. Actually it had seemed more like two meals than one. Mrs. Williams—she told us to call her Nikkollette—wasn't just a good cook, but she prepared lots and lots of good food. The table had been almost over-flowing with food—plates and platters and bowls of chicken and fish, steak and salad, peas and corn on the cob, biscuits and dessert. Even more unbelievable than the quantity of food that had been set out was that most of it was gone! Maybe it was a combination of the food being good and all of us working up such an appetite in the gym.

Jerome, Johnnie, Joshua and Mr. Williams were all big guys and they had cleaned their plates and gone back for seconds and even thirds. Not that I should talk. I was working on my third helping of the chicken.

"Now that we've all topped off the tank," Mr. Williams said, "who's up for a little game of Scrabble?"

"Scrabble would be fun," I said. "But I was hoping we could drive the go-carts."

"Riding is fun. Racing is even more fun," he said. "Shall we have a mini-Indy?"

Jerome and Josh both yelled in agreement.

Johnnie was the official starter, and we were all strapped into our carts—Kia, Mr. Williams, Sherea, Josh and me. They were beautiful go-carts—all shiny and polished, nothing like the type you rent at an amusement park.

"Aren't you going to race?" I asked Jerome.

"Can't. I don't fit into those type of carts."

"What?"

"I'm too big to fit behind the wheel of the carts," he explained.

"But if you don't fit, why did you buy them?" I asked.

59

"I got them so that young people could enjoy them and that's what I want you to do—enjoy yourself."

Jerome walked over and squatted down between Kia's cart and mine. He checked my shoulder straps and then Kia's to make sure they were on correctly. Next he checked the straps on both of our helmets, tightening them up a bit more.

"Listen," he said, "I want you both to take the first couple of laps real slow. You have to get to know the curves of the track before you start driving fast."

"Sure."

"Either of you ever do any visualization exercises when you're playing ball?" he asked.

"You mean like seeing it in your mind?" I asked.

"Exactly."

"Sometimes before the game I close my eyes and picture the ball going into the net," I said.

"I do that too, especially at the free-throw line," he said. "You have to do the same thing with the track. You have to be able to picture the lay-out in your mind the way you picture the hoop."

"We can do that," Kia said.

"You can once you know what the track looks like. Imagine shooting at a hoop and not knowing how far away it was, or how high or even what shape it was. Take your time the first few laps and get to know the track."

"We'll take it slow," I reassured him.

"Good, cause I wouldn't want anything to happen to you two. I'll be here waiting for you. Remember, go slow."

He tapped me on the top of the helmet.

"Drivers, start your engines!" Johnnie called out.

I turned the key, and the engine roared to life along with the other carts. I was glad I was wearing a helmet to block out some of the sound.

Johnnie stood off to the side of the track. He held up one hand. Then he started to fold down his fingers—four, three, two, one, and then he pointed to the ground. There was a roar as three of the carts squealed away.

Kia and I slowly started off after them. Josh, Sherea and Mr. Williams took the first turn, and then they rocketed away down a long straight-away that led toward some trees. They made another turn and disappeared from view.

We took the first turn, Kia on the outside, and started along the straightaway. As long as we took things slowly we'd be—Kia shot by me and the gap opened up between us. What was she doing? We were supposed to go slow. Then again, this section of the track was straight, and I'd driven carts a lot in the past. I certainly was a better driver than Kia. I pushed my foot down on the accelerator. The cart jumped forward like it had been stung by a bee, and I eased slightly off the pedal. I'd been on lots of carts before, but I'd never been on one that had this sort of power. Kia continued to open up the asphalt between us. This wasn't going to happen. I pushed the pedal all the way down.

Up ahead, Kia hit the curve and slowed down. I kept on accelerating, picking up speed. I had to hope that this thing had brakes as good as the engine. I hit the curve, pushed down on the brakes and cranked the wheel. The cart slid sideways across the asphalt, the wheels caught, and I slingshot around the corner. As soon as the course straightened I pressed down on the accelerator again, and the wheels gained traction. Rapidly I closed in on Kia. She hit another curve, and I braked and slid in right behind her. She came out of the curve wide—I didn't think she had any idea I was right there.

Up ahead the next curve was to the left. I steered over to her left and started to pass when she veered over, cutting me off! I hit the brakes and steered hard to the right to avoid rear-ending her cart. She slowed down as she got to the curve, and I went wide to avoid contact. I put the pedal to the metal, shooting by her, keeping the accelerator down until the last second, braking and steering into the curve. At least that would be the end of Kia.

I pushed down on the pedal, moving through the straight section and then braking at the next curve and—*BANG*! I was jerked forward in my seat—she'd smashed into my rear end and bounced me forward! If I hadn't had both hands firmly on the wheel she might have forced me right off the track.

Whether it was an accident or on purpose, she wasn't getting by me. I picked up speed. I glanced over my left shoulder—she wasn't there. I looked over the right—she was just back and off to one side. She was smiling! I'd wipe that smile off her face.

I hit the last corner, braking at the last second, cranked the wheel and slid into the corner. As soon as I started to straighten out again, I pushed the pedal to the metal and surged forward. There was another long straightaway, and I pushed the cart probably harder than I should have but as fast as I needed to in order to stay in front of her.

Up ahead were two tight curves. I stayed hard on the accelerator until the last moment, started to brake and—*BANG*—she bashed into me again, jerking my head forward. Unbelievably she started to pass me on the outside. I let my cart go wider and wider until there was no room to pass. The two carts touched, and Kia's cart shot off the track and onto the grass.

She bounced and bumped and slowed down dramatically. I pressed down on the brakes and slid to a stop...was she okay? She came to a stop in a cloud of dust. Quickly I undid my shoulder strap and jumped out of the cart, racing toward her and—she started to drive away! She continued across the grass, slowly moving, cutting the corner of the curve until she edged back onto the asphalt. Then she quickly accelerated and was gone before I could even react. I raced back toward my cart. I knew she'd be waiting at the finish line—a smug smile on her face—a smile that wouldn't last through the next lap, when I was *really* going to show her how to go-cart.

Chapter Six

"Good morning, everybody," Sergeant Push-up said.

He almost sounded cheerful. Maybe he was going to be easier on us today—or maybe he was just looking forward to us doing a million more push-ups.

We were all standing spread out along the baseline. Kia was just beside me. Two down from her was our good friend—we'd found out his name was Jamal. I'd watched as people came in. Lots of different people seemed to know each other. They talked and laughed and played around. Jamal was like us and he didn't seem to know anybody.

"It's good to see that we're all here on time this morning," Sergeant Push-up said. He cast a look at Jerome, who looked down at his feet. I knew it was just an act, but Jerome was a pretty good actor.

"Before we start the warm-ups, Jerome will say a few words," he said.

Jerome walked to the front. "Thanks," he said. "Glad you all came back today. I was hoping we hadn't scared any of you away. The first thing we're going to do today is divide you all up into teams. Each team will have seven players and those players will be teammates for the remainder of the week."

I looked down the line. I had been checking out the players yesterday—figuring out who was good and who wasn't. I knew some of the best basketball players in the world came from the Washington area and I'd been nervous about playing against them. Coming here I'd wondered if we would be good enough, if we could compete. Now I wasn't so worried. There were a couple of players who looked like they were better than us, but we were amongst the best. Our *buddy* Jamal was actually one of the few people I thought had more skill than us. The only thing more remarkable than his skill was his trash talking. It wasn't just Kia and me he gave attitude to. He seemed to tick off a lot of the other kids.

"You're probably wondering how we're going to choose up teams?" Jerome said.

There were nods and mumbles from along the line as people agreed. That certainly was in my mind. The biggest thing I hoped was that Kia and I would be on the same team. It was hard enough knowing only one person. It would be really hard not knowing anybody on my team. It wasn't that people weren't friendly—lots of people had talked to us—but it was different than knowing somebody.

"We were watching all of you yesterday. This morning before you all arrived the coaches sat down and figured out how to divide you into teams," Jerome said. "We want teams that will be competitive and evenly talented. It wouldn't be fair to any of you if one team was much better than all the rest."

"Not fair at all," Johnnie added, "and no fun for the team that would be so much better. There would be no competition, and they wouldn't learn and grow as players."

"So, listen up as I call out the names!" Sergeant Push-up said.

He was wearing that serious, almost scary face, but I knew better now. Underneath that serious surface was a nice gentle man—a father, a grandfather and a great Scrabble player.

He started to call out names. I watched as people responded to their names being called.

"That's the first team," Sergeant Push-up said.

There were a couple of good players on that team, a couple I hadn't noticed—which meant they were probably not too good or too bad—and one guy who was just plain awful.

Sergeant Push-up continued to call out names. A second team was assembled. Again, I could tell they had balanced out the team with kids of different skill levels on it.

"Nick!" Sergeant Push-up called out.

I startled out of my thoughts and trotted over to his side. He looked directly at me and gave me a little wink—he knew that I knew his secret—and I was keeping it. I winked back, and I caught the slight shimmer of a smile start to form before he swallowed it back inside and scowled a little bit harder.

He called out a second name. I spun around to see who it was. I didn't know his name, but

I'd seen him play—he was okay. He walked over and we exchanged a low five. He seemed like a pretty good guy.

Unfortunately that meant one less chance that Sergeant Push-up was going to call out Kia's name. Who was I kidding? They weren't going to put Kia and me in the same group. They'd probably separate people who knew each other so that we'd get to know other people.

"Jamal!" he called out.

I startled in shock. Jamal! No, anybody but him!

Jamal and another kid stepped forward, looked at each other and stopped.

"That's right," Sergeant Push-up said. "There are *two* Jamals in this camp."

Maybe it wasn't going to be him. I looked at the other Jamal. I didn't know anything about him, didn't remember him playing, but he had to be nicer than the Jamal I knew.

Sergeant Push-up looked down at his list. "Jamal *Johnson*," he called out.

"That's me," Jamal—the Jamal I knew—said, and the other guy retreated into the line.

Just my luck.

Jamal swaggered over. He didn't look at me or

the other kid as he went to the end of the line.

Sergeant Push-up called out a fourth name, and the guy came forward. He gave everybody else on the team—including me—some props as he walked over to join us. We were going to have a pretty good team. He called out a fifth and sixth name and the next two people joined us.

"And the final person on this team," Sergeant Push-up said, "...Kia."

Kia jumped into the air. I had to work hard not to squeal like a girl. I had to be cool about this. Cool was important.

Kia came over and tapped my hand and the other guys' hands, and then she spun around, ignoring Jamal.

"Go over there," Jerome said as he motioned to the corner of the gym. "Start getting to know your team while you're waiting for the other teams to be chosen."

We walked over to the far corner. The first team that had been picked was already sitting in a circle underneath one of the rims. I could hear them joking around with each other. They sounded like they were getting along. With Jamal on our team I didn't think we'd be getting along anytime soon.

"This isn't fair," Jamal said with a scowl.

"That's right, it isn't fair," Kia agreed.

Jamal looked as shocked as I felt.

"It's not fair that we have to have *you* on our team," Kia said, pointing at Jamal.

"It's the other way around!" he snapped. "Only one girl in the whole place and they have to put her on my team."

"Girl?" Kia said, sounding confused. She looked down at her hands, and then she pulled some of her hair forward so she could examine that as well. "My goodness!" she shrieked. "I'm a girl! Thank you so much for pointing that out! I never knew!"

Everybody started to laugh—everybody except Jamal, who had probably figured out we were laughing at him.

"Real funny," Jamal said. "But I guess it makes sense that you *are* on my team."

"How do you figure that?" Kia asked.

"They probably put us on the same team, so I could make up for what you couldn't do...like play ball."

"I can play ball," Kia said. "I can play all parts of the game. Not like some people."

"What do you mean by that?" he demanded.

"I watched you play yesterday."

"Girl, you probably couldn't keep your eyes off me," Jamal said with a smile.

"Yeah, must be nice to have a fantasy life," Kia said, and everybody started to laugh. "I figure you don't know what a pass is because I didn't see you make one."

"Shut up, you—"

"What's happening here?" Jerome asked as he walked over.

Everybody shut up. Nobody wanted to answer.

"We were just talking," Jamal said.

"Pretty loud talking," Jerome said.

"We were just trying to figure out how we can work as a team," Kia said.

JYD shot us a big smile. "Aaahhh...now that's the challenge. Do you want to know what the secret is?"

We all nodded our heads.

"Come closer," he said as he lowered his voice and motioned for us to come closer.

We all surrounded him, anxious to hear the secret.

"If I told you how to do it," he whispered, "then it wouldn't be a secret anymore. You gotta figure it out for yourselves."

Chapter Seven

"Hurry up!" Kia screamed. "Run harder!"

Jamal was the last relay runner—last for our team and the last period. Some of the other teams had already finished, but there were still six or seven others running. Jamal was running down the gym, threading the ball through his legs with each step—that was how everybody had to move for this drill. He was gaining on the three closest teams. He was actually pretty good. I probably wouldn't say that to him, and I *definitely* wouldn't say that to Kia.

Kia and Jamal had started the camp not liking each other and it was going to affect our team. As the day progressed, we finished last, or close to last in every event. I think they both wanted to blame the other for our failures. I didn't think either was responsible. Every team had a couple of weak links. Neither Kia nor Jamal were one of those links.

Despite being last, Jamal wasn't giving up. I had to hand it to him. He was gaining, getting closer and closer. As he touched the wall and started back, I could see that he'd made the turn before three other teams. If he could pass just one more team, we could avoid having to do push-ups. I wanted to yell out encouragement, but I knew that would annoy Kia and I didn't want to upset her—well, not right now.

Jamal was digging deeper and deeper, moving faster and faster, getting closer and closer and—the ball bounced against his leg and skittered away from him!

"Ugggg!" Kia yelled at the top of her lungs.

I looked up. Jamal was just standing there, frozen, as still as a statue. Why wasn't he chasing after the ball? The first teams finished—to cheers and screams—while the last place teams all raced past Jamal. Slowly he started to move—at least he was moving now. He walked...no, he sauntered across the floor to where his ball had come to rest against the wall. He stopped over top of it, drew back his foot, and then he kicked it the length of the gym! It flew through the air and smashed against the far wall with a thunderous crash.

The cheering stopped. The conversation stopped. The only sound in the gym was the ball as it bounced back across the floor. He picked up the ball, and then he began dribbling it— slowly—toward where we all stood. Every eye was on him, including the coaches. Their mouths were wide open, as if they couldn't believe what he had just done.

He handed the ball to the first kid in our line, and then he walked to the back.

Sergeant Push-Up walked to the front of the teams. "Five push-ups for the seventh place team," he said, pointing at the group right beside us. "Ten for eighth place. Fifteen for the ninth place team, and finally, thirty push-ups for the last place team," he said, pointing right at us.

"Thirty?" Kia questioned. "It's supposed to be twenty?"

"Did I say, thirty?" Sergeant Push-up asked. "I should have said *thirty-five*."

"Thirty-five?" Kia gasped.

"Twenty for finishing last, plus ten for kicking

the ball and finally, another five for questioning what I just said."

"That's not fair!" Jamal protested.

"Do you want to make it forty?" Sergeant Push-up asked.

"You can make it fifty if you want," Jamal said defiantly.

"Fifty it is!"

Before Jamal could say anything else, Jerome held up his hands. "Time-out!" he yelled. "Everybody who has push-ups to do, finish them off, and then go get a drink and get ready to go home...everybody except this team," he said, pointing at us.

I stood there with my teammates and waited as everybody else did their push-ups and walked away. I wanted to walk away—heck, I wanted the floor to just swallow me up.

"Sergeant Kevin, Sergeant Josh and Johnnie, could you leave as well, and make sure nobody enters the gym. We need some privacy," Jerome said. The coaches all walked away.

"Everybody sit down," Jerome said.

We all slumped to the floor. We waited quietly while everybody else gathered up their things from the bleachers and headed out to the foyer.

I turned around. Jamal was still standing, his arms folded across his chest, a scowl plastered across his face. Finally he sat down. I figured that was his way of doing what he was told but being defiant at the same time.

I leaned back, looked up, way up, to Jerome standing over top of us. From that angle he looked like the tallest man in the world, and the tallest man in the world didn't look too happy. What was he going to say to us?

"I thought you'd like a little privacy while you do your push-ups," he said.

He turned and started to walk away. "That's fifty," he said. "Unless you want to go for fifty-five?"

"No, fifty is fine!" I exclaimed. I spun around and dropped into position and started doing the push-ups.

As I started pumping, I saw Kia do the same and then the other kids on the team—everybody except Jamal. He hadn't moved. The scowl was still planted firmly on his face.

"I'm not going to do no push-ups," Jamal snarled.

"Why not?" Jerome asked.

"It's not *my* fault we finished last."

"You finished last as a team, so you take your punishment as a team."

"Well, it wasn't any of us who fumbled the ball!" Kia snapped as she paused between push-ups.

"The only reason I fumbled it was because you were all so slow you put me in a big hole," he said, pointing his finger at the rest of us, "and I had to try to go too fast to make up for it."

"And does that explain why you kicked it afterward?" she demanded.

"I kicked it because—"

"Enough!" Jerome said, breaking Jamal off mid-sentence. "From both of you." He took a deep breath. "You don't have to do fifty push-ups."

"We don't?" I asked.

He shook his head. "Now you have to do fifty-five push-ups."

"What?" I gasped.

"Yeah, five more for fighting amongst yourselves. There is nothing worse than members of a team fighting with each other."

"But...but...," I stammered.

"What if we don't do them?" Jamal asked.

"You don't do 'em and your team can't play in the games tomorrow."

"We're playing games?" Jamal asked.

"All afternoon," Jerome said. "But you can't play ball if you don't finish your push-ups."

Obviously that got his attention. I knew he didn't like doing drills. He came here to play ball.

"What's the point?" Jamal asked. "We're just going to lose anyway."

"Whether you think you're going to win or lose, you're probably right," Jerome said.

"What is that supposed to mean?" Jamal asked.

"It means," Kia said, fielding the question, "that if you figure you're going to lose, you are going to lose. If you believe you're going to win, you probably will win."

"Exactly!" Jerome said.

Kia smiled. Jamal scowled. Boy, could that kid ever scowl.

"You have to improve your *attitude* if you hope to increase your *altitude*," Jerome said.

Jamal dropped the scowl and looked confused. I was confused as well. I turned to Kia, expecting an answer. She looked stunned too.

"Altitude," Jerome said, answering the confused looks on our faces, "is how high you fly. You need to have a good attitude if you want to fly high. You have to believe."

"I believe," Jamal said.

"You do?" a couple of kids asked in unison. I was shocked as well.

He nodded his head. "I believe we have no chance of winning a game because we couldn't win any of the relay races."

"But a game is different," Kia said.

"How's that?" Jamal asked. "Didn't the relays involve passing and dribbling and shooting?"

"Yeah," she said.

"And aren't those the things that you do in a game...at least the things *I* do in a game," Jamal added.

I had to admit he had a point—a point so good even Kia didn't have a snappy comeback.

"So," Jamal continued, "what's the point in doing the push-ups just so we can play a bunch of games we can't win anyway?"

Jerome didn't answer right away. That surprised me. I expected him to tell us we were as good as anybody else and had just as much of a chance to win and...but that wouldn't have been the truth...and I knew Jerome wasn't going to lie to us.

Finally he spoke. "The push-ups don't have anything to do with anything else. You got to do those because that's just the way it is. Second, I think your team has enough talent it could win...if everybody worked together and played as a team."

Like that was going to happen, I thought, but didn't say. Even if we had enough talent there was no way we were going to work as a team.

"And third, the coaches and I were talking. We're going to be making some slight adjustments to the teams."

"You're going to be changing the teams?" Jamal asked.

"Adjusting them to make sure they're balanced and competitive," Jerome explained.

"Now we're talking," Jamal said. "Which team am I going to be on?"

"You're not going to be on any team if you don't finish your push-ups...that is, if you can handle them."

"I can handle them," Jamal said. "I could do a *hundred* and fifty-five push-ups."

"I think you already have," Jerome said and laughed.

He was probably right. If you totaled all the push-ups we'd already done it would have been that many.

"Just do fifty-five more." He turned to me. "Nick, how many of those fifty-five have you already done?"

"Eleven."

"Not bad. Nick's partway there. Anybody think they can get to fifty-five before him?"

Jamal spun around into position and started to do push-ups.

Chapter Eight

We were all on the floor, stretching and warming up to music. Jerome was working the soundboard. He started to perform in front of us like he was in concert. He'd mentioned last night that it still made him nervous being up in front of people. I couldn't get over the fact that he might be nervous in front of a bunch of kids. He played ball in front of tens of thousands of people and millions if you count the people watching on TV. Then again, I'd played ball in front of hundreds of people and that didn't make me nearly as nervous as making a speech in front of my class. I guess it *was* different. Either way, though, he didn't seem nervous—just good. Maybe when he was through being in the NBA he could be a DJ or rapper.

He was putting on a pretty good show. I was surprised by just how good Jerome was. I guess because I saw him as a basketball player, I hadn't thought of him as being able to rap.

"Not bad," Sergeant Push-up said as he looked down at Kia and me sitting on the floor.

"I think he's pretty good," I said.

"I'm not going that far. Now, if he were performing jazz that would be another thing. Wouldn't mind hearing a little Ella."

"Ella Fitzgerald is pretty good," I said.

He did a double take. "You know Ella Fitzgerald?"

"Yeah—Ella, Louis Armstrong, Miles Davis, Grover Washington. I know all the jazz greats."

He broke into a huge smile. "I'm impressed."

"He gets it from his dad. Nick's dad loves jazz," Kia explained.

"We can't go anywhere in his car without him playing his music," I added.

"And do you like jazz?" he asked.

"I like some of it," I said. Actually I liked a lot of it, but I couldn't say that in front of Kia—that just wouldn't be cool to like your father's music.

"Some of it's okay," Kia agreed. "I just wish he'd play something else some time."

"Like some of that?" he asked, pointing a thumb toward the stage where JYD was performing.

"Some rap would be good," said Kia.

"Be better if *they* played some jazz. Tried to get my boys to take up an instrument when they were little, but it didn't happen," Sergeant Push-up said.

"My father says rap is sort of like the grandson of jazz," I said.

"I think it's more like a seventh cousin, twice removed," he said.

Kia and I laughed.

"I just wish my father would occasionally play something else besides jazz," I said. "But he told me I could play whatever I wanted...when I had my own car."

"Sounds about right," Sergeant Push-up said.

The music stopped and everybody started to cheer.

"Excuse me," Sergeant Push-up said. "It's time to get down to a little business." He walked to the front of the stage and talked to Jerome, who handed him a microphone.

"Okay, everybody, time to stop sitting around and start playing some ball!"

Another cheer went up from the crowd, and we all got up and started to move.

"Do I see people walking?" Sergeant Kevin yelled.

If he did, he didn't now, as everybody started to move twice as fast. Nobody wanted to do push-ups to start the day.

"Before we start to play we're going to make a few changes to the teams," JYD said.

There was a grumbling sound as people reacted and looked around. Some people would be happy to be with new people.

We all sat in rows with our "old" teammates. Jamal sat at the end of our line, separated by an open space on the floor. He was, in his mind, already gone, and the open piece of gym floor wasn't the only thing that separated him from us.

I wondered how many changes there were going to be. I really wanted Kia to stay on my team, but I knew there was a chance we'd be separated. That was the price I'd have to pay to not be on the same team as Jamal...not that he was bothering me that much. It was Kia he was driving crazy. Probably as crazy as she was driving him. Funny, I thought the two of them had a lot in common—not that I'd say that to either of them. If we had played together—really played together as a team—we could have done well. The easiest thing would be if they just traded Jamal for somebody else. The only bad part about that was that I thought he was good. We'd probably be trading down for somebody with less talent but a better attitude.

"When we set the teams, we try to balance the teams as much as we can but sometimes we don't do it right," Jerome said.

"Mistakes happen," Johnnie said from the back, and we all turned slightly around. "The biggest mistake you can make is not correcting what's wrong. Most people can't admit their mistakes and refuse to get on with making it better."

"We're going to make some slight adjustments," Sergeant Josh added. "If I call out your name, you stand up and we'll tell you what team to join."

This was good. If he was just calling out a few names, it was more likely there wouldn't be more than one per team—better odds that Kia and I would stay together...unless one of us was the person being traded.

Sergeant Kevin called out a name, and a player at the far end stood up. He called out a second player who also stood.

"The two of you change teams," he said.

Of course I recognized both guys, but neither had seemed like a real standout. Both of those teams had done okay in the drills.

He called out two more names, and two more players switched teams. It did look like one change per team. That would probably mean one change for our team. What if it wasn't Jamal who moved? What if it was Kia...or me? Things would get pretty interesting if Kia and Jamal stayed on the same team, especially without me there to sort things out if they got nasty. Then again, if I wasn't there I wouldn't have to sort things out. It was up to the two of them to work it through.

Sergeant Kevin called out another name, and the guy sitting right in front of me got up. If I was right and they were only trading one player per team, that meant Jamal was going nowhere...and neither were we. I turned around to say something to Kia but thought I had better not. Talking might cost the team push-ups. I guess it made sense that he'd be the player who was leaving—

he was the worst player on our team, and maybe the worst player in the gym. They were going to give us somebody really good and then—

A second name was called, and the two changed teams. I recognized our new player. He wasn't much better than the player we'd traded. During lunch yesterday, while other kids were taking shots and fooling around on the court, he'd gone up into the bleachers and started fooling around on a handheld gaming system.

He ran over to our team, smiled and nodded as he took a seat. Maybe he wasn't very good, but at least he was friendly.

Sergeant Kevin continued to call out names—again, one player per team. Either he was going to go back for a second pass at each team or—

"There, the teams are now set," Sergeant Kevin said.

I turned back around. Kia looked shocked. Jamal looked angry—real angry.

"Each team will now pick a name, a captain and get ready to play your first game. You have fifteen minutes," Jerome said.

Everybody broke into their teams, some going off into a corner, or off to the side, and others just formed a circle where they were already sitting. Our team gathered together off to the side. We started talking and welcomed our new member—his name was Brandon.

I looked past the circle—Jamal hadn't joined us. In fact he hadn't moved. He continued to sit there by himself, his back against the wall, his familiar scowl plastered across his face. Everybody in our group continued to talk. Was I the only one who'd noticed Jamal hadn't joined us?

"Kia, did you notice that—"

"Just ignore him," Kia said.

"He's on our team," I said.

"Don't remind me," she said.

"But we need him," I said.

"Just more playing time for the rest of us," one of the other guys, Troy, said. I knew it wasn't just Kia and me that Jamal had annoyed.

Two of the other guys nodded in agreement.

"I was hoping he'd be the one traded," Troy said.

"Me too," voiced a second person and a third nodded.

"He's a good player. We can use him," I said.

"We can win without him," Kia said.

I shook my head. "I'm not even sure we can win *with* him."

Nobody said anything. I think I'd said what we had all been thinking.

"If you want him, you talk to him," Kia said.

I shrugged. "Sure."

I got up and walked across the gym floor. All around me the different teams were excitedly talking. The coaches all stood together in their own little group. Hadn't they noticed Jamal just sitting there? Jerome looked at me and gave a subtle nod of his head. They'd noticed but weren't going to do anything about it...at least not yet.

I stopped right in front of Jamal. He didn't even look up at me.

"Not the team changes I was expecting," I said.

He didn't say anything, didn't look up. Maybe a lie was what was needed.

"But I'm glad you're still on my team," I said.

"You are?" he asked in disbelief.

"Sure, you're one of the best players here."

"One of?" he asked.

I bit my tongue. "Can't think of another

player here who I'd rather have on my team, so I'm glad they didn't trade you."

"What was with the guy they gave us?" he asked.

He'd said "us"—that was a good sign. "What about him?" I said.

"You know what he was doing at lunch?" Jamal asked.

"That was him in the bleachers playing with his handheld game, right?"

"Yeah, do you know what he was playing?"

I shook my head.

"Chess. He was playing *chess*."

"I didn't know that. Chess is a pretty interesting game."

"You play chess?" he asked—it sounded more like an accusation than a question.

"I know how to play," I said, "although I really don't play." I needed to change the subject. "You gonna come over? We have to figure out a name for our team."

"Is Losers taken?" he asked.

"We could win...if you were with us."

He didn't say anything. This was better.

"We have to pick a captain," I said. "I can't vote for you if you're not going to play."

"You were going to vote for me?" he asked. He sounded genuinely surprised, but then again, I was surprised I'd said it too.

"Why wouldn't I?"

He looked like he was going to answer with what we both knew to be true, but he didn't.

"Well?" I asked as I offered my hand. He took my hand, and I pulled him to his feet.

Now that I'd convinced him to join the team I had to convince the rest of the team to join him.

Chapter Nine

"We picked a captain yet?" I asked as we joined our team.

"Not yet," one of the guys said.

"How about if Jamal is our captain?" I asked.

"What?" Kia asked. There was no disguising the shock in her voice or in her expression.

"Jamal. I think he should be our captain. He's got my vote. How about yours?"

Kia's mouth dropped open. I knew she wanted to say something, but it was like her brain had frozen. It was rare to see her at a loss for words.

"He's a good player, and he wouldn't mind arguing with the ref if he disagrees with the call." Kia couldn't disagree with that because I think we all knew Jamal didn't mind arguing with any-body.

"And he knows the rules," I continued, trying to think of other possible reasons.

"He does?" Kia asked.

"A whole lot better than you do," he snapped.

Kia scoffed. What he didn't know—and I did—was that she knew the rules inside and out.

"How about a little contest, me against you?" Jamal said.

"What sort of contest?" she asked.

"We ask each other questions about the rules. Winner gets to be the captain. Loser gets to shut up."

"Works for me," Kia said. "How about every-body else?"

People nodded their heads in agreement. I wasn't so sure Jamal knew what he was getting himself into. Kia would be pretty hard to beat, and I didn't think Jamal would take to being beaten by a girl, especially in front of everybody.

"Nick, what do you think?"

"If everybody else agrees, I guess I agree too." Like I had a choice.

Kia reached out and she and Jamal shook hands.

"Who goes first?" she asked.

"I'll ask you the first question. I'll try not to make it too difficult for you." Jamal cleared his throat. "How much time is there in the twenty-four second clock?"

"What?" Kia asked.

"You heard the question, so do you know the answer or not?"

Kia gave a scowl that even Jamal could have admired. "Twenty-four seconds."

"Didn't want to start you off with anything too hard since you're a girl," Jamal said.

"I'll try and return the favor, you know, not asking you too hard a question because you're stupid. Now your question. If there is an illegal defense, how much time is reset on the twenty-four second clock?"

"Twenty-four. And with each successive illegal defense after the first, the clock is reset and the team is awarded one free throw and possession," Jamal said. "Right?"

"Yeah...but who doesn't know that?" Kia asked.

"My turn again. How big is the backboard?" Jamal asked.

"Six feet by three and a half feet," Kia said

without hesitating. "My turn. You know the restricted half circle under each rim?"

"Of course," Jamal said.

"How far is it from the basket?" Kia asked.

"Four feet. Enough of the easy stuff. How *wide* are the hash marks on the court?"

This was the first question I hadn't known the answer to. I looked at Kia. Her expression was as solid as stone.

"Two inches," she said.

I looked at Jamal. He nodded.

They went back and forth, asking and answering each other's questions. It was starting to look like they both knew *all* the rules. I had to admit that I was starting to gain respect for both of them. I wondered if they were feeling the same thing?

"Are free throws awarded on double personal fouls?" Kia asked.

"Nope," Jamal said. "Do double persons count against team fouls?"

Kia didn't answer right away. "Ummm...no," she said, but she didn't sound very confident.

Jamal reluctantly nodded.

Kia breathed a sigh of relief. "Okay, let's stick with fouls. How many team fouls are allowed per period before a non-shooting foul becomes a free-throw?"

"Four allowed. Fifth is where the team gets to take—"

"Five minutes until we start to play!" Jerome yelled out. "Five minutes!"

The way these two were going we'd still be sitting here in five minutes, listening to them ask questions.

"I think Jamal has proven he knows the rules—as well as you know them—so I say let's make him captain and you can be the *assistant* captain," I suggested.

Neither answered.

"Come on, we don't have time for this to go on. All those in favor of Jamal becoming the captain raise your hands."

My hand went up, as did Jamal's and then another player's and another and another, until everybody except Kia's hand was raised.

"Might as well make it unanimous," Kia said and raised her hand as well.

"Now we need a team name," I said.

"My favorite team is the Pistons," Troy suggested. "How about the Pistons?"

"I like the Spurs," another guy said, "and they're a better team than the Pistons."

"We ain't no NBA team," Jamal said. "How about if we just think of our own name...something that is us and not somebody else."

"You got any suggestions?"

He smiled. "I was thinking the Zebras."

"Zebras?" a few people questioned.

He nodded his head. "Black," he said, gesturing to himself and the other four teammates who were black. "And white," he said, pointing at Kia and then me.

"But that's stupid. We could be the Pianos or the Penguins if that's what counts," Kia said.

"Now those names would just be plain stupid," Jamal said.

"And Zebras isn't?" she asked.

"Zebras are at least fast and powerful," another kid said.

"And the basic food group of lions and leopards," Kia countered. "Do we really want to be named after an animal that other animals eat?"

"They can only eat them if they catch them," I said. "If zebras run fast enough, maybe they can avoid being anybody's meal. Maybe that's what we have to do. If we run and gun, we can win."

"So are we the Zebras?" Jamal asked.

"Why not?" Brandon said. "I like it."

"It's better than the Pianos," I said.

"Whose side are you on?" Kia asked.

"I'm on the same side as everybody," I replied. "We're all on the *same* side, the *same* team...the Zebras."

"Two minutes until we get started!" Jerome yelled.

"Let's just go with the name...the name doesn't matter, anyway. We better just go with that name," Kia said. "Let's talk about who plays what position."

"I'm tall," Brandon said, "so I could be the center."

He was the tallest on the team—and, from what I'd seen, just about the most uncoordinated kid in the gym.

"I guess that makes you center," Jamal said.

"I usually play four—power forward," I said.

"I'm a shooter," Troy said. "Usually I'm a three."

"And I can play three or four," one of the other kids said.

"Good," Jamal said. "The four of you can alternate in those three spots. Nick, you start at four, and…what is your name?" he asked the new kid. Jamal hadn't been there for the introductions.

"I'm Brandon."

"Okay, Brandon. You start on the bench," he said, pointing to the new kid. "Maybe you can play a little bit of chess or something."

Brandon looked sheepish but didn't argue. I had the feeling he'd spent a lot more time playing chess than he had playing ball.

"I usually play the one spot," Kia said.

"That's where I play," Jamal said. "Can you play two as well?"

"I can shoot."

"Anybody can shoot. The question is if you can score."

"She can score," I said, jumping in to defend Kia before she could jump in and start a fight. "What do you play?" I asked the last player.

"Either guard spot."

"Good. Then the three of you can play the two guard spots."

"Everybody assemble up at the front!" Jerome yelled out.

I was grateful there wasn't time to argue. Once we got out on the court, working together, I hoped whatever problems we had would fade away.

All the teams walked to the front and sat on the floor in front of Jerome.

"We are going to be doing nothing but playing games today," Jerome said, and a cheer went up from the players.

"Each game will last twenty-five minutes, and then we'll rotate teams," Sergeant Push-up announced.

I looked down the line at the other teams. Some of the teams looked like they had a lot of talent. I didn't know if we could take some of them. Actually I didn't know if we could take any of them.

"Since each team has seven players there will have to be two members sitting off. We're going to make sure there are no arguments about playing time," Jerome said.

"And here's how were going to be doing it," Sergeant Push-up said. "We're going to have you number off—one through seven—and we will switch players at a given signal guaranteeing everybody gets the same amount of playing time."

"As well," Jerome said, "we'll be keeping score in every game and the games will count in the standings."

"We have standings?" somebody else asked.

He nodded. "We're gonna be playing a lot of games all day today and tomorrow morning. Then Friday afternoon will be the play-offs to decide on a champion."

"Does the championship team get anything?" Jamal asked.

Jerome smiled. He turned slightly around. "Show 'em JY."

JY, the mascot, walked onto the stage wearing a New York Knicks jersey. He turned around and it had Jerome's name and number on the back.

"During the year I wear more than one jersey. Each member of the winning team gets a genuine, game-worn NBA jersey."

"Wow," I heard Kia say under her breath as there was a collective gasp from everybody there.

"First things first. We have to list all the teams up on the board. What's your team's name?" Jerome asked the first team.

"We're the Thunder!" a kid yelled out proudly and the rest of the team cheered loudly.

Johnnie wrote the team's name down on a big white board—the standings.

He went from team to team—the usual names were given: Spurs, The Storm, Tigers, The Cobras... how could a bunch of snakes play basketball?

"And the final team?" Jerome asked.

Nobody answered right away. "Um...we're the Zebras," I finally said.

There was no cheer from our team, but there were a whole bunch of questioning looks.

"That's certainly a unique name," Jerome said. He turned to his brother. "I don't think I've ever heard that used as a team name before, have you?"

"It's a first for me too, but I like it," Johnnie said, nodding his head. "Strong, fast, a proud African animal."

"You made a good choice," Jerome said. "Let's give it up for them for making such an original choice!"

Jerome and the other coaches, joined by the other kids started to clap. That was just like Jerome, putting a positive spin on something. I didn't really think the kids thought it was such a great name, but they weren't going to argue—if Jerome Junk Yard Dog Williams thought it was good, it was good.

"Okay, let's play some ball!"

Chapter Ten

We'd drawn for numbers. Kia got number two, which meant she was going to sit on the bench for the first two shifts. I got three. Jamal got four.

I walked over to the bench. "If you want we can trade numbers, and I'll sit out to start," I said to Kia.

She shook her head. "I'm not a power forward, and we're going to need you to play hard because our center isn't going to be much good."

I had to agree. Brandon handled the ball like it was a hand grenade—a hand grenade covered in butter.

"You start," Kia said. "Besides, I wouldn't want to separate you and your new best friend."

"I didn't think I needed a new best friend."

"You might have to think again if you keep acting like a jerk."

"I'm just trying to make things work. Let's just try to get along."

"I'm not the one causing the problems."

"Come on, Nick, let's get going!" Jamal yelled.

I turned around. "I'm coming!" I yelled. I turned back to Kia. "If we play as a team, we might surprise a few people."

"With Jamal on our side, if we play as a team, there would definitely be one person who will be surprised—me."

I was hoping she was wrong, but I wouldn't want to bet any money on it. "We'll see."

As soon as the game started it became clear that Jamal was good—very good—even better than I thought he was going to be from watching him run drills. Maybe he was the best player on the whole court. He had a great jump shot and could drive the hoop and dribble equally well with either hand.

What was equally clear was that I had no idea what sort of passer he was because he hadn't attempted one. Whoever was on the court with him just ran up and down the floor. The only way any of us would do more than just see the ball was when he shot and missed. Once I realized that, I started to hope he'd miss.

Maybe I didn't come to a basketball camp to just do drills, but running back and forth down the court without any hope of touching the ball wasn't much more fun than running laps. In fact, it was more frustrating.

Jerome turned up the music, signaling it was time for a line change. I walked over and took a seat on the bench beside Kia.

"You want to just save us both a lot of time and tell me I was right," she said almost before my bottom hit the bench.

"He can play," I said, not wanting to agree but knowing she was right.

"He's good," she said, "although that isn't helping us much on the scoreboard."

There was a flip board for each game. We were already down twelve to eight. Jamal had scored six of those points.

"Assuming either of us ever gets the ball, let's try to pass it around, work it down low. We have height on this team," Kia said.

Kia had been doing what I knew she'd do—she had been using her time on the bench to scout the other team, figure out their strengths and weaknesses. That was the secret to basketball, thinking through how you could use your strengths against their weaknesses because every team—even NBA champions—had weaknesses.

"I'm pretty sure I can take my man down low," I said. "I've been getting position on him on the inside."

"Now all you need is the ball."

"Jamal comes off next and I go on. Talk to him, try to get it through his thick head that he's not the only one on the team...talk to him...okay?"

I nodded. "I'll try."

"Good. Once you get back on, I'll make sure you get the ball. We'll work the ball around, play like a team...the way a team is supposed to play. We'll show him the things you will have talked to him about."

We sat back and watched the game. Jamal was practically running a one-man show. As soon as he got the ball, he started dribbling without even thinking about passing. The other team had figured things out quickly, and they had a constant double team on him.

"Look for the open man!" Kia yelled.

If Jamal heard her, he didn't acknowledge it—he didn't even look our way...but then again he didn't really notice his teammates on the court, so why would he pay attention to those *off* the court?

A third man came over to pressure him, and he was trapped in the corner. There were two open men—one of them standing right under the hoop, waving his arms and yelling. Jamal tried to dribble out and lost his handle on the ball—turning it over. The other team rushed down the court. Nobody on our team went back on defense, and they had a three on none break for an easy lay-up.

"I can't believe this," Kia said. "You gotta talk to him."

"I said I would so I—"

The music came on, cutting me off and signaling a line change.

"Just do it," Kia said as she got up and walked onto the court.

She and Jamal brushed by each other without exchanging a word or a glance. He slumped down on the bench beside me.

"This is pathetic!" he snapped.

I wasn't going to use that strong a word for

how he was playing but at least he understood that he couldn't—

"Can't win the whole thing by myself," he continued, and my mouth dropped open. "I need some help out there!"

"I...I got some points," I stammered. I had gotten a rebound off one of his missed shots and converted it to a basket.

"I don't mean you," he said. "You're the only guy I got out there who knows what he's doing."

"Kia can play," I said.

He snorted. "Yeah, right."

"She can. Just watch her."

Kia had taken over at the point guard spot, and she easily beat the man trying to press her. She was moving around trying to find an open man. As the defense came forward, she saw our center open, right under the hoop. She threw a perfect pass, and the ball went through Brandon's hands, hitting him on the side of the head and bouncing out of bounds!

"Nice pass," Jamal said.

"It was a nice pass," I said, defending her. "It hit him right in the hands!"

"No point. Didn't you watch him during the

drills? Guy's got no hands. He couldn't hold a ball if it was in a gym bag."

The other team came down and scored an easy basket.

The ball was thrown into Kia, and she started dribbling. A second man came on her, trapping her. She looked up court. There were two people wide open. She threw up a baseball pass. The ball soared through the air and dropped right between them. Neither moved as it bounced out of bounds.

"Either one of them could have had that," I said.

"She should have thrown it to one or the other, but not both."

I realized there was no point in trying to convince him Kia could play. He'd have to see it with his own eyes. Unfortunately with Kia out there without much support there wasn't a lot she could do. The other team was scoring pretty much at will and every time Kia tried to bring the ball up, they put the press in place and she was facing two or even three people. She couldn't dribble out of it, and when she threw up a pass, it just squirted through hands or bounced off somebody and was scooped up by the other team. This game was getting well out of hand quickly. Even when I did get out there, and even if Jamal would come out and work with us, we were probably already too far behind to pull this game out of the fire.

A loud whistle blew, signaling the end of the game. I was glad it was over...well, really the game had been over since about the ten-minute mark when it became obvious that we didn't have a chance to win. We had just lost our sixth game in a row.

It had been an awful day. The worse things got, the less we played like a team. Most of the guys had given up, Jamal hadn't made any passes at all, and Kia had gotten stubborn and stupid, not passing to Jamal and really not passing much to any of us.

This last game had been just plain embarrassing. They hadn't just beaten us, they had run the score up and made all sorts of comments throughout the game—trash talking and taunting us. There had been some words between Jamal and a couple of their players during the game.

The two teams met at center court so we could

shake hands. I was getting really tired of being a good sport—or at least pretending to be a good sport. Pretending was the best I could do at this point.

"Good game," I said as I tapped hands with the first guy and then the second and—there was a commotion from behind me. I turned around. Jamal was in an argument with one of the players from the other side. They were in each other's faces and then Jamal reached out and gave the kid a big push and he tumbled backward! Two other kids from their team lunged into the action, grabbing Jamal, and suddenly Kia jumped in, grabbing one of the players and shoving him backward and—

"That's enough!" Jerome yelled as he came forward, getting in between the two teams.

Jamal didn't look like he wanted to be separated. Jerome practically had to pick him up off the ground to get him away from the other guy. Jamal still struggled to get free but he was wrapped up in Jerome's huge arms and he wasn't going anywhere. The other coaches all rushed over. Jamal stopped fighting and Jerome loosened his grip.

"Both teams, come with me, now!" Jerome yelled.

He walked away, and we dutifully followed. There wasn't a sound except for our shoes against the floor. I looked up. Every other person in the whole gym was silently staring at us. This was not good.

Jerome held open the door to one of the change rooms, and we all shuffled through. I was glad to be getting away from everybody else's prying eyes and ears.

"Sit," Jerome said.

The other team sat down on the bench on one side of the room, and we all took the other side. Everyone sat in complete silence. I kept my eyes on the floor. I didn't know exactly what was going to happen, but it wasn't going to be good.

"Now, somebody tell me what that was all about," Jerome said quietly.

Nobody answered. I took a deep breath. Should I answer?

"Jamal?" Jerome asked.

"Why you asking me?" he said defiantly.

"Because you're one of the captains, aren't you?"

"Um...yeah."

"So?"

He shrugged.

"He started it!" one of the players on the other team yelled before Jamal could say anything, pointing right at Jamal. "He took a swing at me!"

Jamal jumped to his feet, and I thought he was going to rush across the room and start fighting again, but Jerome got in between them.

"Sit down," he ordered, and Jamal slumped back down onto the bench.

"We're here for a discussion. Jamal, did you hit him?"

"I didn't hit him," Jamal said.

I knew that was a lie. Everybody in the whole room knew that was a—

"I pushed him," Jamal said. "But I *should* have hit him."

"They were trash talking," Kia said.

"Yeah, saying how they wiped the floor with us!" Jamal said.

Actually they *had* wiped the floor with us, but I guess that wasn't the point.

"They were disrespecting us," Jamal continued.

"Nothing worse than a bunch of bad winners," Kia said.

"Yeah, exactly!" Jamal agreed.

Strange, the two of them agreeing on something.

"How about a bunch of bad losers?" Jerome asked.

I knew he didn't really want an answer to that question.

"I don't care how it got started," Jerome said, "but it's going to end right here. Nobody is going to be trash talking anymore," he said, looking at the other team. "If I'd heard it during the game, I would have stopped it right there and then. And nobody is going to be putting their hands on anybody else," he said, looking down the line at the members of our team.

No one said anything.

"Now, we're only a few minutes from the end of the day. Everybody head out and get ready to go home...everybody except Jamal, Kia and Nick."

Chapter Eleven

I understood him asking for Jamal to stay behind, and even Kia, but why me? I hadn't done anything wrong. I hadn't pushed anybody, or even argued. All I'd done was try to have everybody get along and play ball together. I was the guy who got Jamal to come back and rejoin the team.

"You three really got your butts kicked out there," Jerome said. "You really took a beating. They made you look bad. Man, I don't think I ever got beaten that badly in my whole—"

"Yeah, we lost," Kia said, cutting him off.

"Do you know why you lost so bad?" he asked.

I figured that was another one of those questions that didn't need to be answered.

"Would you say that I know basketball?" he asked.

"Of course, you know basketball," I said. "You're in the NBA."

"And I know basketball players. I know there is no way that the three of you working together on the same team should be blown off the court like that. Do you know why you lost so bad?"

I knew, but again, I wasn't going to answer.

"You didn't play like a team," Jerome said. "You know there is no *I* in team."

"But there is in *win*," Jamal said.

"And I didn't see any *W* on the standings board," Jerome said. "I saw six games and six losses."

"I played as well as I could," Jamal said. "I scored more than half of the points in every game."

"And how many assists did you get?" Jerome asked.

"Not many," he said under his breath.

"You're right...if you consider none to be not many."

"I got some assists...didn't I?" he asked and looked at me.

I shook my head. "I don't think so."

119

"We can't win if you don't pass the ball," Kia snapped.

"Maybe you shouldn't be talking," Jerome said. "How many times did you pass the ball to Jamal?" Jerome asked Kia.

"Well..."

"You can't point a finger at him unless you point one at yourself," Jerome said.

Kia didn't answer. She looked at the same patch of floor that Jamal was already staring at.

"And what about you, Nick?"

"Me?" I asked in shock. "I passed to both of them."

"You passed the ball, but you also passed the buck."

"I don't understand."

"Did you talk to either of them about the way they were playing?"

"Talk to them?"

"Tell them honestly, from the heart, that they were wrong in what they were doing? Did you?"

I shook my head. "I tried a bit...but I didn't think they'd listen."

"You don't know if they'll listen or not, but

if you don't try, you can't succeed. You didn't try."

We all sat there in silence, staring down at the same piece of floor.

"Can I ask you a question?" Kia asked, finally breaking the trance.

"Of course."

"Why did you put the three of us on the same team?"

"Only girl here and I'm stuck with her," Jamal said.

"I hadn't really thought about that. I don't look at those things, like I don't notice what color somebody is," Jerome said. "I don't see color. I just see character."

"Dr. Martin Luther King said that," Kia said.

Jerome smiled. "I'm impressed."

"He's one of my heroes," she said.

"He's one of my heroes too," Jamal said.

"Mine too," Jerome said. "The reason I put the three of you together is that I thought you'd play well together."

"I guess you were wrong about that," Kia said.

Jerome shook his head. "I don't think I was wrong. Right now you're not a team. If you decided to work together you could *still* be a good team. I'm going to leave the three of you to figure out how to do that."

Jerome walked out of the dressing room, leaving us sitting there. Nobody said anything. I knew if I waited for one of the other two to start talking we'd be there all night.

"What are we going to do?" I asked.

"Isn't that kind of obvious?" Kia said.

"Not to me."

"We have to start working as a team," she said.

"Do you two think you can work together?" I asked.

"I can work with anybody...if I have to," Jamal said.

"I don't think there's any choice. Jerome isn't going to change the teams at this point. Besides, you two already started to work together," I said.

"We did?" Jamal asked.

"Did you notice who was the first person to help you during that fight?" I asked.

"I was too busy being shoved by three guys to notice anything," Jamal said.

"It was Kia," I said.

"It was?" he asked and looked up at her.

She shrugged. "There were three of them. Somebody had to even up the odds."

"But you don't even like Jamal, so why did you do it?" I asked. "Why did you jump in to help him?"

She didn't answer right away. Finally she spoke. "He's my teammate."

"No way I could stand there and take that garbage from those guys," Jamal said.

"Somebody had to tell them to shut up," Kia agreed. "If you hadn't shoved that guy, I would have!"

"Yeah, good for you, girl!" Jamal said.

"Those guys did deserve to be shoved around. After all we can't have anybody going around telling the truth," I said.

"What is that supposed to mean?" Kia asked.

"They were telling us what a joke we were, how easily they beat us. Wasn't the score thirty-five to seventeen? Aren't we a joke?" I asked.

Both Jamal and Kia looked at me angrily, but neither of them said anything.

"Maybe it's time to stop complaining about people *calling* us a joke and stop *being* a joke." I turned to Kia. "Can Jamal play ball or not?"

"He's good."

"How good?"

"Really good," she admitted reluctantly.

"I agree. He's one of the best players we've ever played with. And what do you think about Kia's play, Jamal?"

"She's okay," he said.

"Just okay?"

"Okay...maybe she's the second or third best player on the team."

"And you think you're the best?" Kia demanded.

"Isn't that obvious?" he questioned.

"Both of you stop it!" I said. "Let's stop fighting about what we can't agree to and start talking about the things we all know. Can we all agree that we want to win?"

"I hate losing," Jamal said.

"You know how I feel about losing," Kia said.

"Can we also agree that the three of us are the best players on our team?"

"That's a no-brainer," Kia said.

"Yeah, sure," Jamal agreed.

"Can we also agree that without the three of us working together we don't have a chance of winning?"

They both nodded.

"Then we know what we have to do...starting tomorrow...agreed?"

I put out a hand. Slowly Kia put her hand on top of mine. We looked at Jamal. He hesitated, and then he put his hand on top of her hand. I put my hand on top of his, then Kia followed, and Jamal topped the pile with his other hand.

Chapter Twelve

By the time we got out of the change room the entire gym was deserted.

"Where did everybody get to?" Kia asked.

We hurried across the floor and out the door to the lobby. Jerome was standing there with Johnnie. Everybody else had gone.

"I was wondering how long you three would be," Jerome said.

"Has everybody else gone already?" Jamal asked.

"Everybody."

"But what about my ride?" Jamal asked. He sounded worried.

"Your ride is right here. Me and Johnnie are driving you home."

"That's cool," Jamal said.

"Is my mother here?" I asked.

Jerome shook his head. "I called and told her we'd drive you home. Didn't make sense for her to come and get you when we're heading home anyway."

"Let's get going," Johnnie said.

We headed out of the lobby and into the parking lot. It was empty except for Jerome's big black SUV.

"Nice wheels," Jamal said.

Jerome climbed in behind the wheel, Johnnie beside him, and the three of us got into the back—I sat between Kia and Jamal.

Jerome started the vehicle, and the sound system came to life with some nice beats pumping from it.

"I'm pretty sure I can give you directions to my house," Jamal said.

"No need. I know how to get to your house," Jerome said. "I've known the Jones family for years."

Jones...wasn't his last name Johnson? Maybe they shared a house? Or maybe his last name was different from his mother's or something like that?

We drove along in silence for a while, just listening to the music.

"Do you live close to here too?" Jamal asked me.

I laughed. "We live a long way away. We live in Canada."

"I thought you guys talked funny," Jamal said.

"We don't talk funny," Kia said. "You talk funny!"

"Nobody talks funny," I said, jumping in between them. "We just talk differently, that's all." Nobody could argue with that. There was no question that we had a different accent than Jamal and the rest of the kids at the camp.

"I thought you guys just played hockey up there in Canada," Jamal said.

"Yeah, we play hockey, live in igloos and drive dog sleds," Kia said.

"I know you don't live in igloos, but I just don't think of basketball when I think of Canada."

"You never heard of the Toronto Raptors or a guy named Steve Nash, the NBA MVP?"

"That's right, he's from Canada, isn't he?"

"Yeah, he is," I said, answering before Kia could get into it again. "And while we don't live in igloos or drive dog sleds, we do have a whole lot of guys who become hockey players."

"I watch ice hockey sometimes. It looks like a pretty good game," Jamal said.

"I like hockey," I said. "Not as much as I like basketball, but it's a good game."

"You must like basketball to come all this way to a camp," Jamal said.

"We came because Jerome is our friend," Kia said.

"More like a big brother," I added.

"And that's why we're staying at his house," Kia added.

Jamal's jaw dropped. I knew Kia would like that and had deliberately thrown that detail out to have that effect.

"You're staying with Jerome?" he gasped.

"Sure," Kia said matter-of-factly.

"And we'll have Jamal come on over to the house for a meal some time. Would you like that?" Jerome asked.

"That would be so cool," Jamal said.

"Make sure you get the green go-cart," Kia said.

Jamal gave her a confused look.

"Jerome has go-carts and a big track to race them on," I explained.

Jamal's confused look gave way to one of

amazement. But then again, it *was* pretty amazing.

Jerome slowed down and made a turn off the main street and into a neighborhood. The houses were big with lush lawns and beautiful flower gardens. This was like our own neighborhood, except richer. I had to admit—to myself—that this wasn't the type of neighborhood where I expected Jamal to live. He just seemed like more of an inner-city kid.

Jerome made the next turn. He slowed down and pulled over to the curb in front of the house. It was like something out of movie—a big beautiful house with a white-railed porch along the front and a tree with a swing on the lawn.

"How long have you lived here?" Kia asked.

"Not long...thanks for the drive...see you tomorrow."

"Yeah, see you tomorrow," I said.

Jamal climbed out of the car and walked up the path toward the house. We sat there and watched until he climbed the steps, crossed the path and opened the front door. He turned, waved, and then he disappeared inside.

"He lives in a really nice house," Kia said.

"It is a nice house in a nice neighborhood,"

Jerome said. "A lot different than where he used to live."

"So he and his family just moved," I said.

"Not his family," Johnnie said. "Just Jamal. He lives here with his foster family."

I suddenly felt awful—sorry for him and sorry for giving him such a hard time.

"I didn't know," I mumbled.

"How could you?" Jerome asked. "But they're good people, the Joneses; we know them through our church. They asked if Jamal could come to the camp. They thought it might help him work through some of the anger he's feeling."

He was pretty angry, but maybe now I knew why. I couldn't imagine what it would be like to live someplace else, away from my family and with strangers...even if they were nice people.

"Jamal really doesn't know anybody else at the camp except you two," Jerome said.

"Is that why you put the three of us together? Because we didn't know anybody else?" Kia asked.

"That was part of it," Jerome agreed.

"What was the other part?" I asked.

"Like I said, I thought you'd work well together and make a good team," Jerome said.

"And you *could* be a good team if you played together," Johnnie said.

"We will be a good team...starting tomorrow," Kia said.

"Jamal feels pretty alone. He needs to feel that there are some people on his side...and I know you two are on his side."

I didn't say anything. We hadn't been on his side. He had been a royal pain that we would have loved to have gotten rid of. We'd all be trying harder tomorrow.

Chapter Thirteen

"Team meeting," I said. "We need to talk before we start."

There were only six of us—one of our players, Trevor, hadn't come this morning. I really understood why somebody wouldn't want to come for the final day. It hadn't been fun yesterday. Losing never was fun. But today we weren't going to lose—at least not as much—and maybe it would be more fun. Secretly I wished it had been Brandon who didn't show up, but he was there, bright and early, ready to go. I had to hand it to him, he wasn't discouraged despite how badly he played—despite how bad the whole team was doing.

"Look," I said to start, "we all know that

yesterday was a bad day. Today is going to be different."

"Are we going to lose by more?" Clifton asked.

"We're not going to lose at all," Jamal said.

"Yeah, right," Troy said.

"He's right," Kia said. "We're not going to lose because we're going to play as a team."

"First things first," I said. "Who's going to sit off first?"

Brandon and Troy put up their hands to volunteer.

"No, it's going to be me," Jamal said.

"You?" Kia questioned, sounding shocked.

"Yeah. You start off, set the tone, and then I'm on for the rest of the game."

"That makes sense," Kia said. "I'll go off second and then Nick third."

"Hands in the middle," I said as I put my hand out. One by one, hand by hand, everybody put their hands on top of each other's.

"Yesterday is gone," I said. "We can't fix what happened."

"Yeah, just forget about it," Kia said.

"No, you're wrong," Jamal said, shaking his head defiantly.

Were they going to get into another fight before the first game even started?

"There's no way I'm going to forget about it...I can still taste it," said Jamal. He looked around the group from person to person. "And none of you should forget it either. Remember it so we don't let it happen again."

"He's right," Kia said. "Let's not forget what happened but use it. We aren't going to let that happen today, right?"

"Right," Troy said, and Brandon and Clifton mumbled in agreement.

"I can't hear you!" Kia yelled.

"Right!" we all yelled back.

"That's better! On three...break...one, two, three—"

"BREAK!" we all yelled.

I started away when Jamal grabbed my arm. "Play hard, man, play like you *hate* these guys!"

"But...but..." I shrugged. I didn't hate anybody here.

"Didn't you hate losing the way we did yesterday?" Jamal asked.

"Of course," I said.

"Then use that!" Jamal said. "Have a great game now!"

Jamal walked over and sat down on the bench while I walked onto the court. Sergeant Kevin was at center, holding the ball, waiting. He was our ref for the first game.

We tapped hands with everybody on the other team—a final show of good sportsmanship before the tip-off. They seemed like nice guys. I knew I couldn't play like I hated them because I didn't. But that wasn't going to stop me from playing hard, though. I did *hate* the way we played yesterday.

We lined up. I was just off to one side, waiting for the tip. Brandon had a little bit of height on their man. The ball went up, and he tipped it back to Kia. I broke toward our basket and Kia threw up a pass—right into my waiting hands—and I put up an easy lay-up for our first basket!

There was a loud scream from the sidelines—it was Jamal! He was up on his feet, whooping and cheering, waving his towel in the air. As Kia ran back up the court, he reached out his hand, and they exchanged a hand slap. I was so shocked I almost stopped running.

"Come on, Nick, hustle back!" Kia yelled, and I kicked it into gear, running back to take my spot on the left side of the key—we were running a two-three zone.

The other team came up the court. They looked relaxed, confident. Who could blame them? They knew our record from the first day. Then again, they'd only won one game yesterday themselves, so they were nothing special.

They passed the ball around the perimeter, trying to set up an open shot. Kia jumped forward, knocking down one of the passes. She raced up the court, grabbed the lose ball, leaving everybody on both teams behind. She put the ball up for a lay-up and we were ahead four to nothing.

"Too easy!" Jamal yelled out. "Too easy!"

It was a little early to be trash talking, but I thought he was right. This game wasn't going to be a challenge.

Jamal threw up a shot. It bounced off the backboard, hit the front of the rim, went up into the air and then it rolled around before dropping for a basket. I had expected it to drop. The way he'd been playing this game he could have kicked the ball and it would have dropped in for two points. He'd played well in our first game of the morning, a convincing win, and then even better in our second—a closer win—but he'd been unbelievable in this game. And, we'd needed him to be that good. The team we were playing had only lost two games yesterday and they were really good.

I looked up at the clock. It wasn't the game clock, but the clock that would signal lunch. It was three minutes to twelve. I knew that if we wanted to start the play-offs on time this afternoon, we'd need to start lunch on time. All we had to do was hold onto our three-point lead for another three minutes and we'd win.

"Spread!" I yelled.

Kia knew what I meant, although nobody else had any idea. It was a play our rep team used to kill time. Each person spread apart and to the outside so we could pass the ball back and forth without trying to score. We didn't need to score.

I moved up to the top and Kia threw me the ball. I dribbled away from the key—away from their zone defense. I continued to dribble, not moving toward their net. Their players—all in their positions in the zone—just watched and waited. They'd be waiting a long time if they expected me to come inside. I passed over to Kia who was on the other side, just as far away from the basket and from their players.

Slowly their zone started to shift open, and Brandon slipped in behind them. He raised his hand to show how open he was. If we were trying to score, that would have been perfect. We weren't trying to score. We were just trying to waste time. Besides, I didn't think he could catch the ball and score unless everybody on the other team was in their dressing room.

Kia passed the ball to Jamal. Did he understand what we were trying to do?

"Jamal!" I screamed. "No shot! No shot!"

For a split second he looked confused, and then he nodded in agreement. He tossed the ball back to Kia and cut to an open spot. She passed the ball back to me, and I dribbled and put a pass back to Jamal and—a loud whistle blew, sounding the end of the game! The morning was over, and we'd won all three of our games.

We were now three wins and six losses and ready for the play-offs to begin. Maybe we wouldn't win it all, but we certainly weren't going to be anybody's joke anymore.

Chapter Fourteen

The six of us sat off in the corner, together, away from the other teams. We were eating our lunches and talking strategy. I was mostly just talking. I was too nervous to eat much.

"I think we should try to go man-to-man to start," Kia said, again.

"That won't work. We have to stay with zone," Jamal replied, again. "Even if we could do it right—and we can't—we'd burn ourselves out before we got to the finals."

"The finals?" Kia questioned, suddenly sounding very serious. "Do you really think we have a chance of getting to the finals?"

"Why not?" Jamal asked.

"There are some good teams...teams that beat us yesterday."

"Nobody beat us yesterday. We beat ourselves. After the three games today is there anybody here who doesn't think we can get to the finals?" Jamal asked.

Nobody answered. Maybe they agreed with him and maybe they just didn't want to say anything.

"I don't want to get to the finals," Kia said.

"What?" I questioned.

She shook her head. "I don't want to get to the finals. I want to *win* the finals."

Jamal reached out and gave her a high five. "Okay, is there anybody here who doesn't think we can win the finals? Nick?"

I startled at the mention of my name.

"You haven't said anything," Jamal said. "Do you think we can take it all?"

I didn't answer right away. "I think that if we play the way we did this morning we have as good a chance as anybody else...maybe better."

Just then Jerome came walking up and stood behind us as we sat on the floor.

"Some good games this morning," he said.

"We played pretty good," I answered.

"Looks like maybe I was right all along," Jerome said.

"Right about what?"

"Right about this being a pretty good team."

"Nope," Jamal said, "you were wrong. We aren't a pretty good team, we're the *best* team here."

Jerome burst into a big smile. "I'd be more than willing to be wrong."

"So how are the play-offs going to work?" I asked.

"One loss eliminations. You lose and you're out. The team that finished first plays the tenth place team. Second place team plays the ninth place team."

"We finished seventh," I said. "So that means we play the...the..."

"The fourth place team," Jerome said. "I think that's the Thunder team."

"Oh...we played them yesterday. They beat us by twenty," I said.

"Wrong," Jamal said. "We beat ourselves by twenty. That team is in for a real surprise this time around."

"So if we beat them—no *when* we beat them—then they're eliminated and we go on to play again, right?" I asked.

"After the first round five teams are left. The top team remaining from league play gets an automatic berth in the finals while the four other teams play off for the other berth."

"And what happens to the teams that are eliminated?" I asked.

"Yeah, we need to know that because we're not going to be seeing it ourselves since we're not going to lose any games," Kia explained.

"You said it, girl," Jamal agreed, and the rest of the team nodded and cheered along.

"Looks like your whole team is in agreement. The teams that are eliminated play games against each other until the finals when everybody, as well as parents and anybody else who wants to, can watch the final game."

My stomach suddenly felt a little swell of uneasiness. I wanted to be there playing, but it would be a lot easier just to be sitting and watching rather than being watched.

"So all we have to do is win four games and we're the champions," Kia said.

"Just four games," Jerome agreed.

"That doesn't seem too hard. We won three games in a row this morning. We just have to repeat that plus one. Piece of cake."

"I don't know about any cake, but I know

you better get yourselves ready. Your first game starts in five minutes."

We won the tip, and the ball went right to Jamal. He started dribbling, and instantly the other team sent three men right at him. They were going to triple team him like they had in the game yesterday where they'd beaten us. Jamal tossed the ball up to me—completely open under the net. I took the ball and put in our first points.

The members of the other team looked surprised. From what they'd seen they really hadn't expected Jamal to pass to anybody. It was pretty clear that the best thing we had going for us was that the other teams hadn't figured out that we were playing differently now. With any luck, by the time they figured it out we'd already have such a big lead that they wouldn't be able to come back.

Play after play we'd passed the ball around, sharing the touches and sharing the points. Jamal had actually gotten to the point where he was passing up shots he should have taken so that he could pass off. He seemed to be getting more of a charge out of getting an assist than getting a basket.

Regardless, it was working. We had a healthy lead and it seemed like with each passing moment we got more confident and the other team got more frustrated. I could tell it was hard for them. They had expected to just roll over us again, and when it didn't work out, they started pressing more and more. When that didn't work, they began bickering and blaming each other. The more we played like a team, the less they did. There was still more than half the game to play, but it was over.

I looked at the board. Five teams had been eliminated. Five remained. The first place team—the team that had killed us, the team that we'd gotten into the shoving match with—had won their game and were now guaranteed to be in the finals. They all sat off by themselves in the bleachers, laughing and joking around, hardly paying any attention to the other kids or who had won or lost the other games. They were confident, but why shouldn't they be? They hadn't just beaten our team badly, but had won every single game against every team, all by double digits. Now they had the next hour off, while the remaining four teams fought it out to decide who would play against them.

"Five minutes until the next games begin!" Sergeant Push-up yelled.

"The second games feature The Heat versus the Pistons on the far court, and The Zebras take on the Cobras on the center court!" said the announcer.

I looked up at the board. The Cobras had finished second. They had only lost one game—to the first place team—and had beaten us fairly easily. This was going to be a harder game. Not impossible, just harder. We were ready.

The Cobras were a good team—and a smart team. They had expected us to play the same way as we had in our loss. When we didn't— when we played like a team—they reacted quickly and started playing us straight up. Jamal was a good point guard, and he and Kia worked really well together. Both of them could dribble, shoot and pass when the rest of us were open.

The music came up, signaling us to substitute players into the game. It was my turn to go off. I sat down—no, I practically collapsed onto the bench. I was tired, really tired and I felt like I needed the rest. Right now I thought we could really use that seventh man—our player that hadn't shown up today.

In the beginning it had been an advantage because it meant more playing time for Kia, Jamal and me. That extra playing time had helped us win that first game, but now it was starting to wear us down. Even if we won this game, how would we be for the next game, or the finals? We were running ourselves down, and the team that we'd be playing in the finals—if we made the finals—was going to be completely rested.

I couldn't think about that. I had to keep my mind in this game. I took a big drink from my water bottle, put it down and got up off the bench. I needed the break, but I didn't want my legs to lock up on me.

"Keep running!" I screamed as our team came back on defense after scoring a basket.

Kia picked up her pace, but she looked really tired. She was due to come off next.

"Close game."

I looked up. It was Sergeant Push-up.

"Closer than I'd like," I admitted. "They're a good team."

"There are two good teams out there playing in

this game. There won't be any loser out there," he said.

"Maybe no loser, but there will definitely be a winner—the team that scores the most points— and I hope it's us."

"Could be. You're up by one point with not much longer to play."

The words had hardly come out of his mouth when the Cobra's point guard put up a three-point shot and it dropped!

"Hardest part is that, while your team and the Cobras are playing each other hard, the first place team is resting, and watching."

"Watching?" I asked. I looked over to the bleachers.

Four members of the team were sitting and watching our game, while the other three members were watching the other semifinal. They were scouting the teams so that they knew what to expect. That was smart, but it wasn't good— at least not good for us. Up to this point we'd had the element of surprise on our side and that had been good for at least a few baskets at the beginning of each game. They now knew that we were a different team—a real team—and they'd be waiting for us.

The music swelled again, signaling a final substitution. Kia trudged over to the bench.

"Play 'em hard," Kia said as we tapped hands and she sat down and I stood up.

It was our ball.

"In bounds the ball to me," Jamal said to me under his breath. "And then head for the basket. I'm going to put up a three-pointer. If I miss, I need you to get the rebound."

"We only need two to tie," I said.

"But we're not trying to tie. Have confidence."

I nodded. "Just do it. If you do miss—and I don't think you will—the rebound is mine."

"Come on, you guys, let's get playing," Johnnie said. He was also watching our game.

I tossed the ball in to Jamal, and he started to dribble down the court. I ran to get into position under the hoop.

Out of the corner of my eye I noticed Johnnie looking down at his watch. I knew what that meant. We were almost out of time.

"Hurry up!" I yelled at Jamal.

He dribbled around his man, stopped, squared up just outside the three-point line and shot. The ball went up, a beautiful arc, and hit the rim and bounced off! I jumped up, grabbed the rebound and went to shoot when I was smacked hard on the hand. The ball went up and somehow dropped.

"And one!" Johnnie yelled out. "That's a foul!"

I rubbed my hand. He had really given me a good shot.

"Nice basket…are you okay?" Jamal asked.

"I'm good. How much time is left?"

We looked at Johnnie, who had heard the question.

"None," he said.

"None?" I asked.

He shook his head.

"That's perfect!" Jamal exclaimed. "You make the shot and we win, simple as that."

"Yeah, simple." I walked over to the line, and Johnnie handed me the ball.

"And since time is up, everybody go back to your benches," Johnnie said.

I stood there, waiting, while every player on both teams retreated to the sidelines. I was standing there all alone. Then I looked farther down the gym. The other game had ended. It wasn't just the two teams watching, it was everybody—all the players and all the coaches.

I had to just relax, not think about the audience around me. I went through my regular, foul-shooting routine. I spun the ball ever so slightly in my hands, bounced it twice, took a deep breath and...it wasn't helping. My stomach did a flip.

This wasn't the usual situation, so I needed to do more than just the usual. I thought about what Jerome had talked about out there on the go-cart track. I needed to visualize the ball going into the hoop. I closed my eyes and pictured the whole thing in my mind, the ball in my hand, bringing it up, pulling it back and then letting it fly, up and into the net. Perfect.

I opened my eyes and shot the ball. Up and in, nothing but net!

Chapter Fifteen

A cheer went up from the crowd, and as I raised my hands in celebration I was knocked over from behind as my entire team tackled me and piled on top. I felt like I was being smothered by bodies.

We finally disentangled ourselves, and Jamal helped me back to my feet.

"That's what I'm talking about!" he screamed. "I knew you were going to make it, I just knew it!"

I looked over at the other team. They looked shocked and sad and disappointed. I always hated that there had to be a loser in a game that was that close.

"Come on," I said. "We have to congratulate them on a good game."

I walked over and started shaking hands with the players on the other team. Every player, without exception, offered their hand and congratulated us on winning, a couple of them telling me how well I handled the pressure of taking that last shot. They were being good losers, and I wanted to make sure we were good winners. That game could have gone either way at any time.

"Five minutes to the next game!" Sergeant Push-up yelled out. "Five minutes!"

I turned to Kia. "Who are we playing?"

"I don't know."

We looked up at the big board. The third place team had been beaten by the sixth place team. We were playing a team we'd beaten this morning!

"That's fantastic!" Kia screamed. "We can take them, and they know we can take them."

"Let's not be overconfident," I warned. "We just beat a team that beat us before."

"That was before we became a team. All we have to do is play our game, our way, and we're going to win," she said.

I didn't argue because I thought she was

right. All we had to do was play within ourselves, play together, and we could beat
them.

The game started just the way we thought it
would. We played confidently: passing, shooting,
hustling and working like a team. We'd taken an
early lead and just kept building it little by little.
By three-quarters time we were up by fourteen
points. The game was ours to win and the only
way we could lose was if we got stupid, and that
wasn't going to happen.

Just after half we'd started to slow the game
down. That was always a good thing to do when
you were winning, but it was now even more
important. We had another game to play, and
while we'd been running around all afternoon, the
team we'd be playing had been resting. Resting
and waiting and watching.

When it was my turn to sit down, I had one eye
on the game and a second on our opponents for
the finals. They were sitting together, watching,
talking—one guy was even taking notes. There
was no way that they wouldn't know our game
inside and out. They'd be watching for the inside
lob to me, Jamal dribbling and then pitching it

back out to Kia for a three-ball, and Kia and me using a pick-and-roll to free one of us up. This was going to be a hard game to win. Actually I'd almost given up on the idea of winning. I just wanted to make sure we could make it a game and not get blown out.

The music came on loud to signal a substitution. I got up off the bench reluctantly. I really was tired and could have used a few more minutes of rest—not a good sign with another game still to come.

Sergeant Kevin blew his whistle to signal the end of the game. We all came together to congratulate each other. Funny, it was a lot more low key than the last game. I guess that was partially because this game had really been over for a while and partially because we knew what winning meant. We had one more game, the finals, against the best team in the place, a team that hadn't lost to anybody and had blown us away—a team that had been resting most of the afternoon while we were wearing ourselves out to try to get this far.

We formed a line at center court and walked past the other team, tapping or shaking hands, offering comments. They were pretty good about losing and more than half of them wished us good luck.

We walked over to the bleachers and sat down together to rest for a few minutes before the next game started.

The other team was already out on the court at the far net, warming up. They'd been sitting so long they needed to warm up. Not us. We needed to lay down, maybe have a nap.

"How are you guys feeling?" Jamal asked.

"Good," Kia said. "A little tired."

"My leg is hurting," Brandon said.

"You play ball, you get hurt, you play through it," Jamal said. "Right?"

Brandon nodded his head dutifully. My left leg was sore as well, but I wasn't going to mention it.

"We played pretty amazingly just to get to here," I said. "We're short a man and we've still managed to win six straight games today."

"Six down and one more to go. Seven wins and we're the champions. I really want that game jersey," Jamal said.

"Yeah, that would be great if we could get them," I agreed.

"What do you mean, *if*? We win, we get the jerseys, right?"

"Yeah…of course," I mumbled. "I just know it's going to be a hard game."

"Nobody said anything about easy."

"They're really good," I said.

"And like we're not?" Jamal questioned.

"Yeah, we're good. It's just that they're good and rested."

"That just means we're going to have to dig deeper," Jamal said.

"Yeah," Kia agreed. "Just listen to what our captain has to say and we'll be fine."

He reached out and gave her some props.

"It's simple," Jamal said. "We'll just have to keep doing what we've been doing and we'll win."

Keep doing what we've been doing…suddenly it hit me.

"No," I said, "you're wrong."

"What do you mean, I'm wrong? You don't think we can win?" Jamal questioned, and that familiar scowl returned to his face.

"No, I think we can win, but we won't if we keep doing what we've been doing. We have to do it differently."

"What do you mean?" Kia asked.

"They've been watching our last two games. They know what to expect. We have to surprise them by being different than what they expect. We have to do something new."

"What do you have in mind?" Jamal asked.

"We have to start off with a press, a full court press."

"But if we're already tired, a press will make us even more tired," Kia said.

"Then we have to do what our captain said and dig a little deeper. Thirty minutes and then we can rest for the whole weekend."

"We can dig deeper, but we haven't practiced a press," Jamal said.

"We'll just go simple. You and Kia double on the ball carrier, and I'll lay back at half to look for a bad pass. We won't do it much, just to start the game and then a few times during the game. Do you think they've been figuring we'll put on a press defense?"

"Why would they?" Kia said. "Nobody has put on a press during any of the games."

"That's my point. Let's just try it."

Jamal slowly nodded his head. "We can

try. Besides, once we get back we can rest a little when we get into zone coverage."

"Okay, that's another thing. We should start with man-to-man."

"Are you crazy?" Kia exclaimed. "Are you trying to burn us out before the first quarter is over?"

"I'm not talking about the whole quarter. Just start man coverage to go with the press. Then go back to a full zone. Just mix it up so they don't know what's coming."

Jamal started laughing. "That will drive them crazy."

"That's the idea. They expect us to come out and do the things they've been preparing for. They also expect us to be tired, and they're hoping they can run us into the ground. Instead we're going to run them into the ground."

"Do you know what they also expect?" Jamal asked. "They expect us to roll over and play dead. They figure that we'll just be happy to get to the finals and that we don't expect to beat them."

I suddenly felt guilty. That was how I was feeling.

"I could have lived with losing to any other team here except these guys. Look at them," Jamal said, pointing down to the far end of the court. "They figure the game is over, they have the better players, they know us better, they're better rested, and that even *we* believe we can't beat them." He paused. "Forget it. I didn't come this far to lose, to have them rub it in my face one more time. If we don't beat them, there was no point to any of this. We might as well have lost all our games if we don't win this one. I'm not going to let them win."

"There's one more thing," I said. I turned directly to Jamal. "You know all those great passes you've been making, the way you've been setting people up and not taking shots?"

"Yeah," he said proudly.

"You have to stop."

"What?" he exclaimed.

"You have to stop. You need to take that ball, drive the hoop, put up shots and keep doing it."

"But we got this far playing as a team," Kia said.

"We're still going to play like a team. We need Jamal to be the best player out their, drain their defense, make them double and even tri-ple team him. Then, and only then, does he pass off. And then the rest of us are going to beat them. Okay?"

Jamal didn't answer.

"To help our team win you have to be the best player out there on either team. Your team needs you to be a star, and I know you can do it," I said.

He smiled. "I can do it, and then I can put the ball back into other people's hands."

"That's what we need," I said. "Now, hands in. Let's show 'em how to play ball...on three... break."

Chapter Sixteen

The stands were packed. All the other teams and coaches, except for Sergeant Push-up and Sergeant Kevin, were in the stands. The two of them stood at mid-court. They were the refs for this game. A lot of parents, including my mother, Jerome's mother, his wife and all his girls, were also there. It was crowded. I was feeling nervous as I paced the sidelines, waiting to be introduced. That was another change from the other games. Each one of us was being introduced individually by Johnnie, standing up on the stage, microphone in hand.

The other team had already been introduced as well as the first three members of our team. It was obvious, judging from the crowd's cheers, that we were the team they were pulling for. I knew people liked cheering for the underdog. I also knew our opponents had beaten everybody sitting in the stands and hadn't been particularly nice about it.

Kia's name was called out and she skipped out onto the court, hands held high above her head, as big cheers rolled out from the bleachers.

Gabrielle jumped to her feet. She was waving a big sign that said *Go Girl!* She and Kia had become good friends over the last few days. They were both confident, determined and far from shy.

Kia tapped hands with everybody on our team, and then she went over and shook hands with both refs.

"And now, playing at power forward for the mighty mighty Zebras...Nick the quick!" said the announcer.

Head down I trotted onto the court as the crowd cheered. It was almost as loud as they had cheered for Kia and definitely louder than for anybody on the other side. Gabrielle was on her feet again. I liked the support but not the Go Girl! sign that she was still waving.

I slapped hands with our team members, and then I went over to shake hands with the two refs.

"Good luck," Sergeant Kevin said. He was being very serious and formal—like a good ref should be.

"Feeling nervous?" Sergeant Push-up asked as I shook his hand.

I was tempted to say no, but that would have been a lie.

"Yeah, a lot," I said.

"I know where you're coming from," he said. "Jerome is always nervous before he starts to play."

"He is?"

"For sure. Big game, big audience. I always figure if you're not nervous you're really not ready to play."

"Thanks, I'll try."

"Do you think your team can win?" he asked.

"I guess we can."

"You guess? Just remember, if you think you can do it, then you can. Can you win?"

"We can win," I said but didn't sound very confident.

"Remember, attitude leads to altitude," he said.

I remembered Jerome saying those words to us—is that where he'd gotten them from...from his father?

"I'll ask you again," he said. "Do you think you can win?"

I shook my head. "No, I don't think we can win...I *know* we can win."

He broke into a laugh, and I trotted back to our team as Johnnie introduced Jamal.

The crowd got even louder, although along with the cheers there were a couple of boos. Jamal had annoyed more than a few people during the course of the camp.

He came on, quietly, businesslike, his head down, not looking at the crowd or responding to them at all. He tapped hands with everybody, and then he went off to shake hands with the refs.

Kia leaned in close. "Is this going to work?"

"Only one way to find out. Let's play some ball."

Two members of the other team walked down to our end.

"Good luck," one of them said.

"Thanks," I said, "and good—"

"Because you're going to need lots of luck if you think you have a chance against us," the other team member said.

"Not luck, a miracle," the kid behind him snapped, and they both started laughing as they walked away.

"Don't waste your breath arguing with them," Kia said. "We don't talk to trash, we take it out."

They stopped laughing, but Jamal started.

Almost all the kids at boot camp had been friendly to us and everybody else. Not these guys. They thought they were better than everybody else. I guess, judging from the game scores, they were better players. That didn't mean anything about them being better people, though.

"Just forget about what he had to say," Kia said.

"No," Jamal countered, "don't forget. Use it. When you feel tired, just dig down and remember that smirk, that laugh, that attitude. No way I'm letting that guy get the last laugh."

A whistle blew, and we went out to center court.

We knew we couldn't get the tip. Their center was the tallest guy in the camp and had springs in his legs. We were just going to try to figure out where he was going to tip it to and get there first.

Everybody lined up. Sergeant Kevin tossed the ball up, and as the two centers jumped up, we all shifted into different positions. The ball went into a gap that Kia had already filled, jumping in front of their waiting player. He was too stunned to move as she whipped the ball over to Jamal. Instantly there was a player on him. What were they doing? They hadn't gone back to zone but were playing man-to-man as well! I hadn't expected that, but I should have. Man-to-man was the best type of defense to put on a team that was already tired.

Jamal started dribbling. I wasn't worried about him. One man wasn't going to be enough to stop him. He cut to the left, and I realized his man had his head down, trying desperately to stay with him. I stopped, planting myself right in the path he was going to go, prepared to set a pick. Jamal looked up and saw me standing there. He cut in, just brushing by me, and his man, head down, slammed into me full force. I held my place, and he bounced back, and then his legs buckled and he fell down! There was a roar from the crowd.

Jamal continued dribbling, uncovered. He closed in, faked a pass to Kia and then went in for a lay-up, putting us in front. The crowd cheered again.

I reached down to offer a hand to Jamal's man sitting on the floor. He brushed my hand aside and jumped to his feet. He shoved me backward, and Sergeant Kevin stepped in between us.

"That was a foul!" Jamal's man screamed.

"That was a pick. Perfectly clean and legal pick," Sergeant Push-up said.

"I guess he's never seen one before," Kia said, "at least not that close up and personal."

Without thinking, I started to laugh. Sergeant Push-up gave me a stern look, and I swallowed the laugh.

"Let's play some ball," Sergeant Kevin said. He threw the ball to one of their players waiting by the baseline.

"Press," I said to Kia, just to remind her.

The ball was tossed in, and Kia was all over Jamal's man. As he turned to try the other side,

Jamal joined in. He swallowed his dribble, and they converged on him, smothering him. Desperately he tried to look for a man to pass to, but his whole team had raced up court. He threw up a desperation pass, and I leaped up, grabbed the ball and started back down court. We were three on one. I stopped, faked a shot, and put the ball over to Jamal. He dribbled, took his steps and dropped in another easy basket.

"Way too easy," Jamal said as he picked up the ball and handed it to one of their men.

Once again we put the press on. They threw the ball in, and again the carrier was swarmed by both Kia and Jamal. Stubbornly he tried to dribble out of double coverage, but they had him trapped in the corner and he had to pick up his dribble. Desperately he tossed the ball back to the man who had thrown it in, but before he could move Jamal was all over him and he fumbled the ball away—it just ticked off Kia's hand before it went out of bounds. The two players started to talk—no they started to *argue*—about who had done what wrong.

"Nice to see," Kia said. "Always good when the other team is fighting with each other."

"Let's keep up the pressure—press again," I said.

Jamal and Kia were ready for the ball to come in again. By this time the other team had figured things out and the ball was tossed up court to another player. I immediately went after him—he was my man. Kia and Jamal came running back and got on their men. We were now playing man-to-man defense, and, just like with the press, they weren't expecting it. They tried to run a play, expecting lots of space up top as we settled into a zone. Instead we were all over them, and they scurried around trying to find an opening that wasn't there. Finally they put up a shot—high and wide, clanging off the backboard and into Brandon's hands. To my complete shock he grabbed the ball with both hands and held onto it. He sent the ball over to Kia who turned and passed to Jamal, who was streaking down the court, uncovered. It was a perfect delivery and he dropped another easy lay-up.

Three shots, three lay-ups, six-point lead. This *was* way too easy.

Jamal scored our first twelve points before they changed defenses and started sending double coverage after him. As soon as that happened, he started passing to the open man, and we got easy uncontested shots. We put the press on and off repeatedly, as well as switching back and forth from man-to-man to zone coverage. It kept them off balance and helped us build a solid early lead.

Unfortunately, keeping them off balance and getting an early lead didn't mean keeping them off the score sheet. They had height on us, and once they stopped fighting amongst themselves and started playing as a team, they chipped away at our lead. This team also had the one advantage we couldn't overcome—they were rested and we were tired. Little by little they chipped away at our lead until finally, with only a few minutes left in the game, they'd pulled even. Then their best shooter hit one from behind the arc and they pulled away to a three-point lead.

There were times when I knew what was going to happen, and what I had to do to stop them, but my legs just wouldn't do what my head told them to do. Even worse than running out of energy, we were almost out of time. There couldn't be any more than a minute left in the game.

"Time-out!" Kia yelled.

We trudged over to the bench and huddled together.

"Well?" Kia asked.

"Well, what?" I said.

"What are we going to do now?" she asked, looking directly at me.

I shook my head slowly. "I'm not sure what we should do. They're pretty good."

"They're not better than us!" Jamal snapped.

I gestured over to the scoreboard. "Three points better than us. I don't have any more ideas."

"Okay," Kia said, "in that case tell us what we *shouldn't* do."

"What?" I asked, hearing but not understanding.

"Tell me what we shouldn't do if we want to win. What should we avoid?"

"Well, we can't afford to sit back. They have the lead and all they have to do is kill time," I said.

"So you're saying no zone defense, we have to go back to a press and man-to-man again," Kia said.

"That's what we should do," I agreed. "I just don't know if it will work...nobody has the legs for it."

"I'm beat," Kia said, "but if we don't at least try, they win for sure, so we have nothing to lose. Right after we score we go into a full court press. Everybody is up and contesting for the ball."

The scorer's table signaled time, and we broke from the huddle. Jamal grabbed me by the arm. "We can still win," he said.

"I know," I said. "I haven't given up."

I in-bounded the ball to Jamal. He started up the court. They were back waiting in a zone defense. I set-up low-post and sealed my man off. I held up my hand, and Jamal sent in a perfect pass. Before I could move, a second man came and dropped down into coverage, and I was double-teamed. I pitched it out to Kia, who rotated it over to Jamal. He put up a shot, and the ball dropped in for two points! The crowd screamed and yelled, kids were pounding on the bleachers, and all three of Jerome's daughters were jumping up and down, waving their signs.

"Press! Press! Press!" I screamed.

I looked at the clock. It was ticking down to under twenty seconds. This was it.

They threw in the ball. I lunged forward, but it shot just past my outstretched hands. Instantly the ball carrier was covered by two men. He passed

173

off, and we converged on that man. He tried to dribble, but we locked him down, and he had to eat his dribble. He passed the ball off to another man, who was swarmed by two other players and—

"Time violation!" Sergeant Kevin yelled.

We'd done it! We'd pressed them so hard that they couldn't take the ball over half-court in time. It was our ball!

Sergeant Push-up handed me the ball, and I walked over to the sidelines. I looked over at the clock again. It was down to eight seconds left. More than enough time for a shot, but not enough for a second chance. Either we scored and we won, or we missed and we lost. One more chance.

I'd just throw the pass into Jamal and hoped he could put up a winner. I was just getting ready when I realized they'd gone back to man-to-man coverage and two of their men were on Jamal. They weren't going to let him get the ball.

"Stack!" I yelled, and our team formed a line right in front of me while the other team scrambled to try to get in position to cover.

"Break!" I screamed, and everybody broke off in different directions, two of their players trying to stick to Jamal's side and a third following Kia.

"Jamal!" I yelled, and every eye turned to him.

I faked a pass and then turned. Brandon was alone under the net. I threw the pass in toward him—not too soft or it wouldn't get there, but not too hard either or it would go through his fingers. The whole world slowed down as if I was watching a slow-motion replay. I could see the ball gently spinning, the seams rotating, and then the ball hit Brandon square in the hands. It slipped partway out of his grip and my heart rose into my throat, but before it could escape he grabbed it. He hesitated, and then he pumped and put the ball up, through the air and off the backboard. It hit the rim, rolled and rolled and rolled, and then it dropped in!

Chapter Seventeen

The gym was practically empty. It had taken over an hour for us to get our jerseys, for the coaches to say their final words and for all the kids to have a final picture taken with Jerome, JY the mascot and the other coaches. I sat on the bench, rubbing the numbers on my new jersey—my NBA worn-in-a-real-game jersey. It was big enough to be a dress on me...heck, it was big enough to be a tent on me.

I thought about the way the game had ended, the way the crowd had reacted and the ceremony, as we received our jerseys and camp certificates. It all seemed more like a dream than something that had really taken place.

Sergeant Push-up took a seat beside me. "That was a pretty gutsy play, sending the ball in to Brandon."

I shrugged. "He was open."

"He was, but if he had missed, you know who they would have blamed, right?"

"I know, but it was still the right thing to do. Nobody was expecting it."

"Least of all Brandon. Did you see the look on his face when you threw the ball toward him?"

"I was too busy looking at the ball."

Sergeant Push-up laughed. "The boy looked like a deer caught in the headlights of oncoming traffic. For a second there I thought he was going to try to get out of the way of the pass."

My stomach flipped just thinking about it. "But he didn't. He caught it and scored and we won."

"Your team won long before that," he said. "Didn't see anybody on the other team laughing once the game started. You earned their respect before you earned the victory."

"Respect is good. Winning is even better."

He shook his head. "No, it isn't. I'd rather lose and be respected than win a game in a way that caused me to be disrespected. Your team did win and earned respect." He held out his hand. "Congratulations, I'm proud of you, son."

My hand disappeared into his big mitt. Funny, I was happy about winning, and happy about getting the jersey, but I was even happier about what he'd just said.

I got up from the bench. My mother was off in one corner talking to Jerome's wife and his oldest daughter Sherea. Kia and Jamal were playing with Giselle and Gabrielle down at the far end of the gym. Jerome was the only other person still in the gym. He was pushing a garbage can along, bending down and picking up empty drink bottles and wrappers. He was cleaning up the gym. The NBA celebrity basketball player was cleaning up the gym. Somehow I wasn't surprised.

I walked over to his side. "Need some help?"

"I could definitely use some help."

I climbed up into the bleachers and grabbed a couple of half-filled bottles. I tossed the two bottles. One went straight in the can and the second hit the rim and bounced off. Jerome picked up the rebound before it had hardly hit the floor and tossed it in.

"I guess I could have got all the kids to pitch in and clean up, but everybody seemed so happy I wanted them to leave on a high," Jerome said.

"Everybody was pretty happy," I agreed. "You could just leave this to the caretakers to clean up."

He shook his head. "The caretakers didn't make any of this mess. It's my boot camp, so it's my responsibility. You don't have to help if you don't want to."

"No!" I wanted to help. "It is the least I can do to make up for all you did for Kia and me this week."

"That was just my pleasure. Besides, look how much you gave back," he said, gesturing down to Jamal.

"He's an okay guy," I said.

"Even better, I think he's going to *be* okay. This was a big step." He paused. "You think you might be staying in touch with Jamal, you know, letters or e-mail or calls?"

"I'd like that. I better find out how to contact him before we drop him off...we are dropping him off, right?"

"We are, but you'll have time tonight. Jamal and his foster family are joining us for a little victory dinner at the house."

"That's great."

Jerome tossed some more trash in the can.

"Do you know when I knew you'd won?" Jerome asked.

"When Brandon tossed in the basket," I said.

"Up until it dropped through the mesh, I didn't think we were going to win.

"No," he said. "I knew you'd won the minute you sent that pass to Brandon."

"I wasn't sure he'd make the basket or even catch it to begin with."

"Neither was I," Jerome admitted.

"But you said you knew we'd won?" I questioned.

"I didn't know if you'd win the *game* until the basket dropped, but I knew you'd *won* as soon as you passed to him."

"I'm not sure I understand what you mean."

"Let me see if I can explain it. What was the difference between all the losing yesterday and all the winning today?"

"That's easy. We started playing as a team."

"And who is on your team?" Jerome asked.

"Well there's Kia and Jamal and..." I stopped. I knew exactly what he was saying. "There were six members of my team, not three."

He nodded his head. "Three of you were good enough to get you to the finals."

"But not enough to win in the end," I said.

"Winning isn't just about what shows on the scoreboard when time expires." He paused.

"Don't get me wrong. Basketball is my passion and my job, and I play to win, but I know there's more to life...and I think you know that too. Today you showed what a winner looks like."

He put a hand on my shoulder. He was right. This felt better than winning the game.

"Now," Jerome said, "I just have one more question."

"Yeah?" I asked, hesitantly, wondering if I could answer this one.

"Did you come over here for the conversation or are you actually going to help clean up?"

"I was cleaning up...I will clean up...I..."

Jerome broke into a gigantic smile, and he winked at me, and I smiled back. I knew I was a winner...and so was he.

Eric Walters is the author of forty-five books for children and young adults, including the nine books in the best-selling basketball series featuring Nick and Kia.

When not writing and visiting schools, Eric enjoys spending time with his family and playing and coaching basketball. He has such a fertile imagination that he still thinks he could give JYD a challenge if they played another game of one-on-one. Eric lives in Mississauga, Ontario, with his wife Anita and their three children, Christina, Nick and Julia. The character Nick is based on Eric's son Nick, whose team, the Mississauga Monarchs, have twice won the Ontario Championship. Many of the other characters in this series, including Jamie, Mark, Jordan, Paul and Tristan, are his real teammates.

Johnnie Williams III is a social entrepreneur and inspirational speaker who travels both locally and internationally. When speaking to youth and adults of different nationalities, ages and gender, he is the type of person who takes the extra step, goes the extra mile and connects with people. Johnnie has just created the website, www.changetheworldmovement.org, to make a world of difference by promoting the good deeds of others around the world.

Teachers love the way Johnnie speaks at the level of his audience and redirects youth admiration back toward them and other true role models. Students love the fact that his presentations are unscripted, upbeat and filled with real-life examples. Many school boards have benefited from his effective youth program concepts and youth outreach strategies. Johnnie stays connected with the youth he encounters through a personal email address established for their questions and requests for advice: justaskjohnnie@aol.com.

Jerome Williams is a recently retired NBA athlete and full-time advocate for youth and the community at large. Jerome studied sociology at prestigious Georgetown University, where he received a B.S. degree and the Raymond Medley "Student Athlete" award.

Jerome has incorporated many of his sociological theories and practices into his daily life as he did throughout his NBA career. The results have made a tremendous impact in the lives of millions of youth as well as the hundreds of NBA players who elected him to a four-year term as vice president of their players' union. His professionalism and character have become a solid part of his personal brand.

Off the court he has become the fan favorite in each of the four NBA cities he has played, paying attention to the needs of fans, friends and family. The media has loved Jerome for his infectious personality, charisma and often animated demeanor. The NBA has just named Jerome one of its Community Ambassadors, which requires him to travel the world promoting teamwork and the life principles found within the game of basketball.